WILD WEST DETECTIVE

Rance Dehner, an operative for the Lowrie Detective Agency, pursues a wanted killer to the small town of Hardin. After bringing down his opponent in a gunfight, Dehner discovers the man was in town to murder Leona Carson — a penniless teenaged girl with a baby. Seeking to discover why anyone would hire a gunman to dispose of Carson, Dehner finds himself dodging bullets from an onslaught of professional killers — whilst uncovering the shameful secrets of Hardin's leading citizens.

Books by James Clay
in the Linford Western Library:

REVEREND COLT

JAMES CLAY

♦

WILD WEST DETECTIVE

Complete and Unabridged

LINFORD
Leicester

First published in Great Britain in 2014 by
Robert Hale Limited
London

First Linford Edition
published 2016
by arrangement with
Robert Hale
an imprint of
The Crowood Press
Wiltshire

A catalogue record for this book is available
from the British Library.

ISBN 978–1–4448–3004–0

Published by
F. A. Thorpe (Publishing)
Anstey, Leicestershire

Set by Words & Graphics Ltd.
Anstey, Leicestershire
Printed and bound in Great Britain by
T. J. International Ltd., Padstow, Cornwall

This book is printed on acid-free paper

*For Kennerly and Patrick:
Two trailblazers who bring a touch
of glory to untamed lands.*

1

Strange things are said to happen on the night of a full moon. People turn into wolves. Sweet and shy women take a knife to their husbands. Men of peace wantonly commit murder.

Rance Dehner was not a superstitious man. Still, he was observant and had noted that on nights when the moon was a round orb there were a lot of odd occurrences.

On this night of a full moon, Dehner was following a killer, Curt Tatum. Tatum had tethered his horse to a tree and was heading somewhere on foot. This was definitely full moon stuff; there seemed to be no place for Tatum to go. Dehner followed on foot at a safe distance.

Suddenly, no distance was safe. Curt Tatum moved out of the wooded area into a wide space dotted only sparsely by a few bushes and trees. The killer was moving toward a line shack, cautiously, like a mountain lion stalking prey. The shack had one window at the front, now beaming a faint glow of kerosene yellow. Tatum darted over to the side of the cabin, safely out of the light. Dehner had no idea who was inside that shack, but it was no friend of Curt Tatum.

Dehner had experienced several previous run-ins with Tatum and knew he couldn't trail closely behind him without cover. No matter how quietly he moved, the killer would hear him.

For a moment, Dehner considered bushwhacking his prey. The man was a wanted killer. No one would argue if he brought Tatum in with a bullet in his back. He quickly rejected the notion. He couldn't do that.

Tatum wheeled around quickly, sensing a presence behind him. One hand hovered over the gun nestled in a holster on his right side. He stared intently at the newcomer, then spoke in a voice filled with mockery. 'Well, well.

Rance Dehner. Thought you and I parted company for good back in Dallas.'

'Yeah, Curt, you crept up on me from behind. Pistol-whipped me good; I took a couple of weeks to recover.'

'You coulda' shot me from behind just now, why didn't you?'

'Company policy.'

Both men were trying to size up the strange situation. They were about to have a gunfight that would leave one of them dead and they both knew it. The moonlight left their faces in partial shadow. A slight twitch of the mouth or eyebrows would not give anything away.

'That company of yours, Pinkerton ain't it?' Tatum took a step forward as he spoke, trying to appear casual. The killer was a fast draw but his accuracy was faulty and the first shot had to count.

Dehner pretended not to notice. 'No. I work for Pinkerton's competition, the Lowrie Detective Agency.'

Curt Tatum wanted to take another

step but decided to hold off. 'Ain't that the outfit owned by that limey?'

Dehner saw his opening. 'Some Brits came over here to start a ranch. They give jobs to hard-working cow punchers. Bertram Lowrie started a detective agency and gives jobs to lazy huckleberries like me. But Lowrie does have some standards. He'd never hire a cowardly snake who'd attack a man from behind!'

'Why — ' Tatum went for his gun; Dehner matched his movements. Both men fired at almost the same time. Tatum's shot went wide; Dehner's went into his opponent's stomach. Curt Tatum began to stagger about, gun still in hand.

'Drop it, Tatum, I'll only say it once.'

The gunman hung on to his weapon. Even wounded, Curt Tatum was a very dangerous man. Dehner's second shot took the killer down.

Tatum's body lay still, his gun now positioned only inches from his right hand. Dehner moved with caution and his Colt drawn until he could feel for a pulse on the gunfighter's wrist. Confident that Tatum was dead, Dehner turned his head toward the strange sound coming from the shack.

A baby was crying.

Dehner again used caution. He crept around the shack and approached the door on the side without a window. He tapped gently on the door.

'Go 'way!' The voice sounded female and scared.

'I won't hurt you. I'm a detective. I need to talk with you, just for a few minutes.'

The baby's crying became louder. The woman's voice turned into a near scream. 'Go 'way!'

Dehner holstered his Colt. 'I'm coming in.' The detective opened the door slowly, stepped into the shack and faced an old Winchester, which was pointed, eye level, at him.

'Don't you move no more. I'll shoot. I really will.' The girl sounded very young. Her clothes were old but clean, a description which could also apply to the inside of the shack and the blankets on the cot, the shack's one piece of furniture except for a small table that stood beside it. The kid had done everything she could to make an old abandoned line shack safe for her child.

Dehner couldn't spot any food. 'When was the last time that baby was fed? When was the last time you had anything to eat?'

'You never mind. Git!' The girl's body was shaking.

Dehner held up both palms in an effort to calm the girl. There was an element of self-defense in the move. That old rifle could probably go off easily. 'I don't want to cause you any trouble.'

'What are you doin' here?'

'Point that gun down and I'll tell you.'

She lowered the gun, revealing a pretty face marred by paleness and red-streaked eyes. Her long dark hair was turning stringy through neglect. Dehner figured all the care the girl had to give went to her baby. He pegged her age at about fourteen.

'My name is Rance Dehner.'

'I'm Leona Carson.' The sudden propriety seemed to confuse her. Leona looked toward the crying infant. 'His name is Samuel.' Hostility again returned to her eyes. 'Why are you here?'

'Like I said, I'm a detective. I trailed a gunslick to this place, an owlhoot named Curt Tatum, ever hear of him?'

'No.'

'Do you have any idea why he was here?'

'Did you kill him?'

'Yes.'

'Then what difference does it make?'

Dehner decided to pull back. He spoke quietly. 'We need to get you into town.'

Leona's face contorted, she pressed her lips together. 'I want nothin' to do with Hardin, Texas. Someone there tried to kill me. Me and my baby.'

'What?'

'Last night, Samuel and me was sleepin' at Riley's Blacksmith and Livery. We was in a back stall. Riley never bothers to close the place up. Late in the night I heard someone sneakin' around.'

'What do you mean, 'sneaking around'?'

'Sounded nothin' like a customer lookin' for his horse or bringin' one in. This jasper was searchin' for somethin' besides a horse. Turns out that somethin' was me.'

'What happened?'

'I left the stall to see what was goin' on. A man grabbed me, took a look at my face, then tossed me on the ground and pulled out a pistol. I screamed. Del Burgess, he works at the livery. He came runnin' with a rifle. Whoever it was fired a shot in front of Del. Del fell down and the man ran off. He was fast. Del said he placed that shot perfectly, in such a way to make him stumble and fall.'

Dehner spoke quickly. 'Curt Tatum could have done that.'

'Who?'

'Curt Tatum, the hired gun lying dead out in front. He could have killed your friend, but didn't. A killing would have brought in the law. Curt just waited for another chance to get at you.'

'How did he know I was stayin' at the stable, or out here?'

'Curt was good at finding things out.'

'But why would someone pay a hired gun to get me?'

'You can answer that question better than I can, Leona.'

The girl fell silent. She glanced at the baby, who was now gurgling instead of crying. 'There's no reason to hurt me. I've got no money, no . . . family. All I got is Samuel.'

Dehner thought the young woman had been about to say, 'no man,' but had used 'family' as a quick substitute. He wanted to ask her about Samuel's father but thought it far too soon. Still, the answer to such questions might help resolve who had hired Curt Tatum and for what exact purpose.

'I didn't see any horse outside. How'd you get here, Leona?'

'Del Burgess brought me. We both thought I'd be safe here. Del gets paid tomorra. He was gonna buy some stuff for Samuel and me and bring it out.'

'Well, now we know you're not safe in this shack. We could both use a few hours of sleep. I'll make camp outside and cook up some bacon and biscuits at sunrise. Then we'll leave for town.'

Leona looked at her baby and then at her hands. 'Do you think whoever sent that Tatum guy after me will send somebody else?'

'I don't know. But you've got to be careful, Leona. Very careful.'

She nodded her head. Dehner nodded back and stepped back out the door. By the bright full moon he could see creatures creeping out of the forested area. They weren't werewolves, just coyotes coming to feast on the corpse of Curt Tatum.

Dehner drew his .45 and fired over the heads of the animals. They scattered back behind the trees. He turned his head and shouted into the shack, letting

Leona know what he had just done.

The detective then holstered his gun and walked briskly toward the corpse. He didn't know the sheriff of Hardin well, but he did know that the lawman could identify the corpse as Curt Tatum and send a letter saying as much to the Lowrie Detective Agency in Dallas. As Dehner recalled, Hardin had a professional photographer who did freelance work for the local newspaper. A picture of Tatum's corpse could accompany the letter. The agency could then collect a fee from its client, the brother of a man Tatum had murdered.

Dehner crouched over Tatum's body and remembered that the killer's horse was still tethered in the wooded area, near the detective's bay. He sprung up and headed for the trees. Technically, his job was done. But he knew he had to find out who was trying to harm Leona and maybe harm her child.

The detective made his way through a narrow aisle that twisted through the woods. No mythological creatures of the full moon attacked him. They didn't need to. The fangs of a very real demon burrowed into his soul.

2

The town of Hardin had already begun its day as Rance Dehner rode in with Leona, who was cradling Samuel, sitting in front of him on the bay gelding. They were riding slow. The body of Curt Tatum lay across his hammerhead roan. The horse, whose reins were tied to a rope and attached to Dehner's saddle, plodded behind them.

Dehner spotted three men weaving out of a saloon and on to the street. Though it was only mid-morning, they all appeared to have been drinking heavily. The three men were tall. Two were overweight: of these, one had a salt-and-pepper beard, and the other had scruffy red hair covering his face. The youngest of the threesome was slim and clean shaven with long brown hair, which reached his shoulders.

The three barflies looked with amusement at the riders, who slowly advanced toward them. Salt and pepper shouted in a loud voice, 'Here comes Leona Carson. That girlie was as pure as the snow, but she drifted!'

The barflies loudly guffawed. Salt and pepper continued his taunt. 'Why, that must be the kid's daddy laying across the hammerhead. They got him hogtied and brung him back for a shotgun wedding!'

The drunks resumed their raucous laughter, doubling over, slapping their knees, and shouting ugly remarks at Leona. Two men emerged from the stage depot, which was next door to the saloon, and stepped briskly toward the troublemakers. As they did so, a woman exited from the depot and began a fast walk down the boardwalk, away from the trouble.

The younger of the two men began to drop back as they approached the jaspers. His companion appeared much older. His well-tended mustache was gray as was the hair that flowed from under his Stetson.

Dehner reined up. He was now a few yards from the escalating trouble. 'Do you recognize any of those men, Leona?'

'The drunk doin' all the talkin' is called Bert. The guy with the red hair is ... Red. The young one is called Jimmy.'

'How about the other two gents?'

'The old man is Earl Whitney,' she answered. 'He and his missus own a ranch outside of town.'

'And the young, well-dressed, man?'

'Will Maltin. He's Mrs Whitney's nephew. Lives in San Antonio but loves to work on the ranch. He comes to Hardin much as he can. Looks like he's gettin' ready to take the stage back home.'

Will Maltin didn't appear to be going anywhere at the moment. He stopped in the street and watched nervously as his uncle approached the three drunks. Earl Whitney stepped in front of the leader of the threesome. 'Bert, move on and take your friends with you.'

Bert took one step backwards, then decided he couldn't back down in front of his buddies. 'Mister high and mighty! Didn't think me good enough to work on his ranch.'

'I fired you because I need men who have calluses on their hands, not booze on their breath.'

Red and Jimmy exchanged glances, and took a few steps to position themselves behind Earl Whitney. The rancher noticed their move and shot a fast glance at his nephew. Will Maltin turned quickly and looked behind him, apparently checking to see if help were on the way. Nobody was coming. Will turned back to his uncle with a look of confusion and panic.

'I think I'll go introduce myself to those gentlemen,' the detective said as he slid off his bay and helped Leona dismount. Samuel remained in her arms.

Will Maltin noticed Dehner approaching but the other men didn't. Bert made a fist and waved it in front of Earl Whitney. 'Old man, it's 'bout time somebody taught ya a lesson!'

Earl Whitney was old but so was the barflies' trick. Whitney ducked and pivoted as Red tried to slam a pistol against the back of his head. He then delivered a hard punch that landed under Red's ear and knocked him down. Will Maltin made a startled cry but otherwise didn't move.

Dehner broke into a fast run. Bert and Jimmy now had Earl Whitney surrounded. Bert held his fists up and moved about like a boxer while Jimmy was going for the Remington strapped to his waist. Dehner tackled the younger man, who then dropped his gun as he collided with the ground.

'Who are you?' Jimmy sounded indignant, as if Dehner had just crashed an afternoon tea.

'A man who likes to even the odds.' The detective picked up Jimmy's gun as he buoyed himself to his feet.

With his two partners down, Bert's

pugilistic motions were becoming more limp. 'Ya ain't worth the trouble, old man!' He shouted loudly, but his bravado was phony and he knew it.

'You ain't worth the space in a jail cell, Bert, but that's where you and your buddies is headed!' Sheriff Amos Santell trotted past Will Maltin, drawing his gun. The woman Dehner had seen running from the stage depot was with him.

'Good thing Mrs Whitney came to get me.' The sheriff nodded at the woman standing behind him, and pointed at Dehner. 'This here is a detective from Dallas. He was in town about a year back. The man knows how to use his fists and a gun. You three jaspers wouldn't have stood a chance.'

Dehner laughed, gave the sheriff a friendly nod, and handed over Jimmy's gun as he kept one eye on Mrs Whitney. The woman put an arm around Will Maltin and seemed to be comforting him. The boy looked embarrassed by the gesture.

Earl Whitney shook hands with Dehner. 'Thank you, sir, for helping me keep those saddletramps at bay until the sheriff arrived. What brings you to Hardin?'

Dehner spoke while watching the sheriff march Bert and his pals off to jail. 'Like Sheriff Santell said, I'm a detective — with the Lowrie Agency in Dallas. We were hired to go after a killer named Curt Tatum: arrest him or kill him. I had to kill him.'

Whitney's voice was grim. 'Yes. I have heard about Tatum. Don't feel too bad about having . . . '

Earl continued on, Dehner half-listening to him as well as to the exchange between Mrs Whitney and Will Maltin. Will's eyes were fixed on Leona, who was standing up the street near the boardwalk. She had walked the two horses away from the ruckus.

'Aunt Rose, would it be OK if I were to talk to Leona for a few minutes?'

The woman's response was uncertain. 'Well . . . what for?'

'I just want to say goodbye. It could be three months or more before I come back to Hardin.'

'Yes, of course.' Rose Whitney's voice still sounded a bit uncertain. 'Leona needs kindness from friends at this time. Go right ahead.'

Will nodded to his aunt before leaving to talk with Leona. To Dehner, the gesture almost looked like a salute. The detective shifted his gaze to Leona. The young woman looked both happy and troubled to see Will approaching her. Dehner wondered if . . .

The detective mentally reprimanded himself. If he was going to help Leona he couldn't wonder if every man she encountered was Samuel's father. The lady may or may not give him that information. If not, he would have to solve the case without it.

' . . . yes, those years in the army taught me a lot — '

'Earl! I hope you are not boring this gentleman with your collection of army stories.'

Earl Whitney laughed but he appeared more chastened than amused. 'I probably am, dear . . . '

Earl introduced his wife, Rose, who shook hands with the detective. 'Mr Dehner, I saw you riding into town with Leona. I hope nothing bad happened to her.'

The detective once again explained his assignment to kill or capture Curt Tatum. Rose's response was immediate. 'You have completed your job. Will you be leaving town soon?'

'No. Not too soon.'

'And why not?' Rose smiled in a sly manner.

'I'm a detective, Mrs Whitney. I don't like unanswered questions.'

The smile broadened a bit and the woman's eyebrows rose. 'Such as?'

'Curt Tatum didn't work cheap,' Dehner explained. 'Why would anyone spend big money to kill Leona? And, since Tatum failed, what does that person intend to do next?'

'You are like a stubborn dog with a

bone, Mr Dehner.' Rose's voice held admiration.

'Guilty as charged.' As Dehner talked with Rose, he took note of what a uniquely attractive woman she was. He couldn't peg her age. The woman's hair was the color of honey and gleamed when the sun hit it. The hair formed an exquisite bowl around her face. That face was perfectly proportioned, with only a few lines at the far corners of her blue eyes; eyes that sparkled with vitality. The woman's dress was proper but still showed off her fine figure.

Will Maltin returned to the group. Rose hastily introduced him as her nephew. 'My brother Bradford is a successful businessman in San Antonio. He expects Will to follow in his footsteps. But, when you are seventeen, life at a ranch seems much more inviting than life behind a desk. Will visits us as much as possible, much to my brother's chagrin.'

Will looked uncomfortable. Dehner felt some sympathy for the lad. Will had frozen and left a man about three times his age to handle those thugs alone. Dehner didn't know what to say to the young man, so settled on a handshake and a, 'Pleased to meet you.'

A stagecoach began to pull into town. 'Earl and I will see Will off.' Rose pointed toward the coach as she spoke. 'Then we have business to conduct. Mr Dehner, could you do us a favor?'

'Yes, of course.'

Rose and her companions stepped toward the boardwalk as the stagecoach drew nearer. She had to raise her voice to be heard over the clamor of the coach. 'Put Leona in a hotel room. Tell Humphrey Chandler, the owner, to charge her room to me.'

Rose's eyes briefly fused with those of her husband. 'I mean, tell him to put Leona's room on the Whitney account. Please meet us for dinner at six tonight at Benson's Restaurant. We have a great deal to discuss.'

'I'll see you then.' Dehner went to rejoin Leona. He briefly glanced backward at the Whitneys who were accompanying Will to the stage depot.

The detective laughed inwardly. He could understand Will Maltin a little better now. After receiving instructions from Rose Whitney, he had felt a bit like saluting, himself.

3

Rance Dehner stepped out of the telegraph office after sending a wire to his boss, Bertram Lowrie, in Dallas. The message had advised Lowrie to expect a letter from Sheriff Amos Santell, accompanied by a photo, affirming that Curt Tatum was dead. Dehner had also included a line stating that he would remain in Hardin to 'tie up loose ends'.

As he made his way down the boardwalk toward Benson's Restaurant, the detective spotted a large number of people lining up in front of a general store. A young man was nailing a sign to the wall beside the store's door.

As he drew near, Dehner could read the freshly painted sign:

VIEW THE BODY OF CURT TATUM
LEGENDERY KILLER!
COST: TEN CENTS.

CHILDREN UNDER 12: FIVE CENTS.
1 NIGHT ONLEY!

A short overweight man with a walrus mustache was sitting at a table in front of Novak's General Store. He was selling tickets and doing a brisk business. The line in front of the store was long and new people were arriving steadily. Sheriff Santell and the young man who had put up the sign were keeping an eye on the goings on. So far, everything seemed peaceful.

Dehner approached the sheriff. He was in the street talking amicably with some folks near the end of the line. 'Yeah, we are doing this for the children. Young'uns need to know that a life of crime will getcha nowhere but dead. So, you folks enjoy yourselves. It's for a good cause.'

The lawman turned around and faced Dehner. 'Howdy Rance, good to have ya back in town. Sorry we couldn't talk much earlier, but — '

'I understand.' Dehner again eyed the

fast-growing line as he and the sheriff took a few steps away from the crowd. 'Ah, Amos, do people really believe that story of yours about all of this benefitting the young?'

'Of course not!' Amos guffawed as he stroked his black beard. Santell was a medium-sized man with stooped shoulders and a beard that always seemed to be dotted with shreds of tobacco. 'But some folks feel a bit uneasy 'bout attending something like this, so I tell 'em it's for a higher cause. That gives 'em an excuse for enjoying themselves.'

Dehner smiled in spite of himself. 'And an excuse for spending their money.'

'Well, yeah, that too. Hope ya ain't angry 'bout us not letting ya in on the profits. I guess ya are entitled to — '

Dehner cut him off. 'I'm not angry. After all, it's for a higher cause.'

The young man who Dehner had spotted earlier approached the sheriff. 'Ever' thing seems to be going smooth, only we're getting some complaints.'

Santell introduced the kid to Dehner as his deputy, Max Chumley. The introduction was swift. The sheriff was obviously annoyed by Chumley's news. 'Now, what's this here 'bout some folks complaining?'

Chumley shrugged in a self-conscious manner. He was a tall, wide-shouldered man, probably a year or two short of twenty. 'Folks don't mind paying Stub Novak a dime to see the body. But they think it's wrong for his wife to be inside the store selling cookies. They say the cookies should come with the price of admission.'

Sheriff Santell pressed his lips together in a gesture of disgust, and then almost spit out his words. 'If that don't . . . people today are just too greedy, always wanting something for nothing.'

'Guess so,' the deputy replied.

'Folks don't realize that after I pay Stub for the use of the store and give the undertaker his cut, there just ain't that much left. People need to use their heads and think these things through.'

'Guess so,' the deputy replied.

Amos Santell's anger was not yet fully vented. 'Bad enough I gotta put up with persnickety folks like the Whitneys — '

The detective interrupted Amos, 'What problems have the Whitneys caused you?'

Santell paused for a moment and looked around him. He may have been checking to make sure there were no problems with the large crowd but it appeared to Dehner that he was making sure the Whitneys were not within hearing range.

The sheriff dropped his voice to a stage whisper. 'Rose Whitney, now she's a real looker, I'll give her that, but she's always talking 'bout civilizing the West. She don't approve of this sort of thing. That's why I'm only doing it for one night. Why, I could have kept this going for at least a week. Lots of folks would come back for a second look, even a third.'

Max Chumley nodded his head. 'I

guess showing the dead body of an outlaw ain't civilizing, but there's not much in the way of entertainment in this town. Somebody should explain that to Mrs Whitney.'

'Somebody beside me will have to do the explaining,' Santell growled.

The deputy's voice took on a forced casualness. 'Ah, Rance, how's Leona doing? I heard 'bout you bringing her into town from a line shack.'

'She's fine. I got some good food into Leona and bought supplies for her and the baby. She's resting with Samuel at the hotel. That's what Leona and Samuel need the most right now — rest.'

Max nodded his head in an officious manner, a sworn officer of the law inquiring about a troubled citizen. 'I don't care what some folks say, Leona Carson is a fine woman.'

He paused and then repeated, 'I don't care what some folks say.'

4

'I'll bring out your food the moment it is ready.' The woman's voice was polite but a tad frosty.

'Thank you, Carol, we're not in a big hurry, and I'm sure the pot roast and potatoes will be well worth the wait.' Earl Whitney spoke in the voice of a peacemaker.

Rose Whitney watched in a chagrinned manner as Carol Benson stalked off toward the kitchen. 'Oh, dear. I'm afraid it will be a while before Carol and I are friends again. And we are on the same church committee.'

Dehner was sitting with Earl and Rose Whitney at a table in Benson's Restaurant. 'What happened?' the detective asked.

'Leona Carson used to work for Stu and Carol,' Rose explained. 'She slept in a back room here at the restaurant. Leona was an excellent worker, but

31

when she began to show they made her leave. She ended up doing chores at Riley's Blacksmith and Livery. Horace Riley let her sleep in one of the stalls . . . as if she were a horse!'

'Now, dear.' Earl's voice continued to be that of a peacemaker. 'Horace did what he could for the girl.'

Rose looked embarrassed; her voice became less intense. 'You're right. Horace is certainly not the problem. Anyhow, while all this was going on, Earl and I were very busy at the ranch. We only came into town on Sundays for church. When I found out what had happened . . . well, Mr Dehner, I do have a temper and I'm afraid I lost it.'

'Is that when you had the falling out with Carol Benson?' Dehner asked.

'Yes. On a Sunday morning yet, in front of the church.'

Dehner continued with his questions. 'How has most of the town responded to Leona's situation?'

The woman paused before answering. 'I'd say it was about half and half.

There are people in Hardin who believe that Leona should wear a scarlet A. Others are more compassionate. Earl and I are staying overnight in town. Tomorrow, we will be welcoming the new pastor for the Hardin Methodist Church. We are hoping that he can be of help in getting the church to be more supportive of Leona. Our current pastor is well intentioned, but he is elderly, frail, and doesn't want to kick up dust.'

'Do you know this new pastor?'

'Only by reputation. Earl and I were in San Antonio visiting my brother and taking care of church business. I met with the Methodist Bishop for this area. He told me Jeremy Lanning is a fine young man who has asked for an appointment in what he calls the 'real West'. He is apparently getting restless with his position in San Antonio.'

'Do you think the church can help to find a home where Leona and Samuel can live for a while?' Dehner asked.

'That won't be necessary.' Rose

stopped speaking as both Carol and Stu Benson brought the food to their table. Stu, a bald, medium-sized man, babbled with an artificial cheerfulness while his wife went about her duties silently. Dehner felt relieved when Stu returned to the kitchen and Carol began to attend to a family who were seating themselves at another table.

Rose continued her earlier thought before she began eating. 'Leona is coming to stay at our ranch. She can help Esther, our cook, and do some cleaning. Of course, we will pay her and provide her with plenty of time to care for Samuel.' The woman laughed lightly as she cut her pot roast. 'I will be able to help some with caring for the baby.'

'Have you talked to Leona about this?' Dehner asked.

'Yes, after you put her up in the hotel and then went to conduct some business. I hope I wasn't being out of line.' The tone of Rose's voice implied she didn't care in the least if Dehner thought her out of line.

Since he had met the Whitneys at the restaurant, the detective had been trying to understand the relationship between Earl Whitney and his wife. Earl's eyebrows had jumped a bit when Rose mentioned that Leona was coming to live with them. But the brows quickly returned to their usual location. Dehner suspected that being surprised by his wife's actions was nothing new for Earl Whitney.

Earl was a man who had, without hesitation, stormed into a fight with three men less than half his age. Dehner didn't doubt that the ranch owner was a king to his ranch-hands. But the king exerted little control over his queen. Maybe he allowed Rose her own fiefdom as long as it didn't invade his.

Dehner dropped his voice to a whisper. 'This is a delicate matter, but do either one of you know — '

Rose interrupted the question. 'We don't know who Samuel's father is and neither does anyone else besides Leona and, of course, the father.' She lifted her eyes to the ceiling and then continued. 'Though, the good Lord knows, there has been plenty of speculation. A few gossips even named Will. The boy did take Leona to a church social and a dance . . .'

Earl dropped his fork. It pinged against the side of his plate as he raised his napkin and suppressed a laugh. 'Oh, come on, Rose.' He put down his napkin and grinned at Dehner. 'I caught my wife with paper and pencil figuring out if it was possible for — '

'Yes, yes, I admit, I did figure out if it was possible for Will to be the baby's father. It is possible, though I doubt it.'

Again, Rose's voice may have conveyed more than she intended. Dehner noticed a certain caustic tone as she talked about her nephew. He wondered if Rose would have found Will more admirable if he had gotten Leona pregnant.

'Will is hardly the only name the gossips have come up with,' Rose continued. 'I suppose every young man in town has been a subject of speculation.'

'Not only the young men!' Earl chuckled as he fussed with his food. 'The names of a few old goats have also been bandied about.'

'Yes, that's true.' Rose sounded irritated by her husband's jovial tone.

Another cheery voice interrupted them. 'Anybody care for a second cup of joe?' Stu Benson hovered over the table holding a coffee pot.

Dehner took him up on the offer. Tonight was Leona's last night in town. She would be harder to get to at the Whitney's ranch. Hardin was a small town with the usual gossips. He had to assume that a lot of people knew about the plans Rose Whitney had for Leona. One of those people might decide to kill the girl while she was still a comparatively easy target.

He was in for a long night.

5

Rance Dehner glanced at the two books that lay on the battered chest of drawers in his hotel room. There was a Bible and a book containing three plays by William Shakespeare. The detective knew better than to open either tome. Those books could absorb him. On this night, he needed to be alert in case anyone tried to harm Leona, who had the room next to his.

The detective checked his timepiece: 2 a.m. He sat in a rickety chair and glanced at the newspaper on his lap. On the front page of a month-old edition of the *Dallas Herald* was a drawing of Rutherford B. Hayes.

Hayes had been elected president two years before in a very acrimonious election. He had lost in the popular vote but won in the electoral college. In an attempt to unite the country, Hayes had announced that he would only serve for one term.

According to the newspaper, things were not going all that well for President Hayes. His attempts at reform of the civil service were being stalled by political opponents who were waiting him out.

Dehner felt that he was waiting someone out, too. A few minutes later, his waiting was rewarded. Cautious footsteps could be heard in the hallway outside. Someone wanted to be very quiet. Maybe it was a polite soul who didn't wish to disturb anybody's sleep.

Dehner suspected otherwise.

The detective moved to the door of his room and slowly opened it on to a dark hallway. He could spot a figure in front of the door to Leona's room. The figure was bent over, apparently feeling under the doorknob for a keyhole.

Dehner could hear the click of a key turning. The detective bolted into the hall and quickly followed the intruder into Leona's room. He grabbed the shadow as it advanced toward the girl's bed and wrapped an arm around its neck.

'Put up your hands!' Dehner snapped.

'Lemme go, I jus' wanna — '

'Put up your hands. Now!' Dehner closed the vice tighter, causing the intruder to choke as he raised his hands.

The detective patted his captive's waist. There was no gun there.

'Lemme go. Cain't breathe. Please!'

Dehner lightened his grip only slightly as he spoke. 'Leona?'

'Yes.' The girl sounded frightened. No surprise. This was the third night in a row someone had come after her.

'Get us some light!'

The sound of a flaring match mixed with that of the intruder's quick breathing as Leona touched a flame to the kerosene lamp on the bedside table. The moment light filled part of the room, the girl turned to look at the baby who had been slumbering beside her. Samuel continued to sleep peacefully. Leona then looked at the man Dehner was releasing from his grip.

'Del Burgess, what are you doing here?!' The girl put her feet into slippers and stood up as she spoke.

Del looked back at Dehner before he nervously faced the girl. 'Well . . . ah . . . I got a right. I ain't workin' now. I work at the livery and sleep there. Don't mean I have ta stay there all the time.'

Del's voice was a stammer and Dehner understood why. Leona looked much different than she had that morning. She was wearing a beautiful yellow nightgown, which the detective was sure Rose Whitney had purchased for her. Good food and a good bath had made her appear less gaunt and pale. The young woman was a striking beauty.

Del looked down as if giving himself a quick once over. He was a large-boned, gawky lad of about sixteen. Brown trousers hung a little too far above his ankles and his checkered shirt was faded. A few pieces of hay protruded from his sandy hair. The light freckles on the kid's face were also a sandy brown.

'I stole the key from the extras. Know where they keep 'em. I learned all 'bout this place the time I worked here for a spell when that big crowd came ta town.'

'I know all that! What are you doing here in the middle of the night?' The anger in Leona's voice was subsiding. Dehner couldn't be sure what was replacing it.

The detective took a few steps to the side, which made him a spectator to the conversation between the two young people. He thought that the best position for the moment.

'Well, I had to come now! You're gonna be gone in the morning.'

'How'd you know that?'

Del threw his arms up in frustration. 'This here's a small town! Ever' one's been talking 'bout how Curt Tatum tried to kill you and ended up dead hisself. When someone heard you was gonna stay at the Whitney ranch, that jus' gave folks more cud to chew on.'

Del pressed his lips together for a

moment and then continued. 'I don't wantcha goin' to the Whitney place. Stay here where I can protect you. The baby, too.'

Leona's eyes instinctively returned to Samuel, to make sure the baby was OK. Then she again addressed Del Burgess. 'A fine job of protectin' you've done so far!'

'I can do a heap lot better than an old man like Earl Whitney.'

Anger flared again in Leona's voice. 'Mr Whitney may be old but he's plenty strong. He took on three jaspers this afternoon.'

Leona took a deep breath and a touch of regret moved across her face. She sensed that she had just wounded Del Burgess's manhood and felt bad for it.

The woman's voice became calmer. 'Del, I'm grateful for what you and Mr Riley have done for me. I really am. But I don't want Samuel sleepin' in a stable. The Whitneys have a whole bunch of ranch-hands. I'll be safe.

Goin' out to the Whitney ranch just makes a lot more sense than stayin' at the livery.'

Burgess made fists with both hands dangling at his sides and then slowly unrolled them. He had been out-argued and was now empty of ammunition. 'Reckon you're right.'

'You know I am.' Sadness laced the woman's voice as if she regretted being right.

'Guess I better get back to the livery,' Del said.

'Guess so.' The sadness remained in Leona's voice.

Burgess turned and walked out of the room. Dehner followed him. They walked down the stairs in silence. Del didn't speak until they were outside on the boardwalk. 'I guess you're Dehner, the detective who killed Curt Tatum.'

'That's me.'

''Preciate you helping Leona.'

'Glad to do it.'

Del Burgess stared at the sky. Nothing up there seemed to make him

44

happy. 'What Leona said 'bout staying at the Whitney ranch was right, sorta. I guess I shouldn't have said what I did about Earl Whitney. But that wife of his . . . '

'Go on.'

Del gave up on the sky and turned his head to look at Dehner. 'Rose Whitney is good-looking and she does good things for folks, real nice stuff but . . . '

'But what?'

'Ever' time she does you something good, it's like she's buying a piece of you.'

Del nodded a goodbye to Dehner and began to walk toward the livery. As he watched the boy vanish into the darkness, the detective whispered to himself, 'That kid is a good judge of character.'

6

Reverend Jeremy Lanning placed the coffee pot back on the spider web that covered his camp-fire. He took a quick sip of java, his second cup for the morning. The pastor then returned to an old blanket he had laid on the ground and his secret sin. He picked up the dime novel, *Callahan's Revenge*.

Buckshot Callahan was his favorite dime novel hero. The pastor glanced at the sky. He had about fifteen minutes before he needed to break camp. His morning Bible reading and prayer were finished along with his breakfast. Now he could allow himself some fun before riding into Hardin and the new responsibilities that awaited him there.

Jeremy was only two pages into Buckshot's latest adventure when he heard approaching hoof beats. He quickly placed *Callahan's Revenge* under his Bible. There was really nothing wrong with a man of God reading a dime novel but . . .

Lanning stood up and watched the horse with increasing interest. Something was wrong. The rider seemed to be bent over and having trouble controlling the animal.

Lanning ran toward the approaching chestnut. He grabbed the horse's reins and placed a steadying hand on the rider. 'What happened to you, friend?'

The answer came in a wavering whisper. 'Outlaws robbed me . . . '

'Are you shot?'

'No. They . . . fired at me to make me stop. After that, pistol-whipped me.'

'Did they get much money from you?'

'Yes. I was carrying a fat wallet. Pretty stupid.'

'I'm being the stupid one,' the pastor hastily replied, 'asking questions, when I should be helping you. I haven't broken camp yet. I can fix you some food and coffee, if you'd like, then take a look at your wounds.'

'Thanks.'

Jeremy Lanning walked the chestnut into the camp. He helped the rider off his horse and on to the blanket. He tied up the chestnut and returned to the injured man, who was partially lying backwards, resting on his elbows. 'My name is Jeremy Lanning. I'm on my way to Hardin to pastor a church there.'

The newcomer smiled. 'Robert Smith is my handle. I'm a lawyer in Hardin. I was on my way back from a meeting in San Antonio when I met up with four hardcases. Thanks for being a Good Samaritan, Reverend.'

Lanning smiled as he replied. 'Just trying to practice what I preach.' The pastor noted that like him, Smith was wearing a frock coat with a Stetson perched on his head. Jeremy gently removed the hat. 'There doesn't seem to be any bleeding.'

'I was lucky. The thieves concentrated on my ribs, if you call that luck.'

'I'll help you take off your coat. There are some bandages in my saddle bags. We can — '

Lanning saw the look of displeasure on Smith's face. He mistook it for pain. 'If you don't mind, Reverend, I'd like a cup of coffee first.'

'Yes, of course.' Lanning turned and quickly moved to the spider web. 'I have a clean cup right here. I believe in being ready for company. You know, in Biblical times hospitality was regarded as vital. People couldn't have travelled without it.' He poured java into the unused cup and returned the pot to its place over the fire. 'I guess things haven't changed all that much.'

When the pastor turned around, Smith was on his feet, holding a gun in his right hand. He reached out with his left and took the cup of coffee. 'Thank you, Reverend.'

Lanning looked stunned. 'I don't . . . I don't understand.'

Smith took a sip of java. 'Tastes good. You make a fine cup of joe.'

The compliment only made Jeremy Lanning more jittery. 'Thanks. I still don't understand — '

Smith shrugged his shoulders. 'Like you said, Reverend, things haven't changed much since the Biblical days. As I remember from reading Genesis, the world has been pretty violent since the beginning of time.'

'Well . . . yes . . .'

The gunman continued to speak as if addressing a pupil. 'A man has to be tough to survive. I learned that the hard way.'

'What do you mean?'

Lanning's captor took another sip of coffee, smiled approvingly, and continued. 'My name is really Ash Carrick. I used to be a lawyer, had a practice in Houston.'

'So . . . ?'

'I took a case involving some powerful interests. I was opposing a team of very expensive lawyers from the East. The only way I could win was . . . well . . . let's say I cut some corners.'

'And you got caught.'

Carrick carefully set the cup on the ground. 'You got it right. Not only did I get kicked off the case, procedures were initiated to have me disbarred.'

'Did you fight it?'

A loud harsh laugh cut the air. For a moment, Carrick lost his gentlemanly veneer and his eyes grew wide with a primitive wildness. 'I fought, all right. But not the way you're thinking. I couldn't have won a disbarment hearing, so I fought a different fight.'

Lanning was terrified. He tried not to show it but his voice began to tremble. 'What kind of fight?'

Carrick fell silent for a moment. When he spoke again, he was back into his mockingly friendly character. 'I discovered that my legal colleagues from the East had a taste for the low life. They would spend the dark hours patronizing establishments in Houston's more seamy districts. I caught up with them one night as they left a saloon. I gunned them down, all three of them dead within less than a minute.'

Reverend Lanning shivered and took a step backward as if trying to escape the horror that confronted him. 'Why do such an awful thing? Killing those men didn't benefit you!'

'Ah, but it did!' Carrick's grin broadened and his left arm began to gesture frantically. He wanted the reverend to understand his point. 'I had never felt so powerful before in my life! I was so in control. The next few days I read the newspapers carefully. I wanted to know everything about those men. Because of me, the head of one of Boston's most prestigious law firms was dead. I also killed the fiancé of a high society debutante as well as a man who was primed to run for the city council.'

The joy in his captor's face overwhelmed Reverend Lanning. For a moment he stared at the killer as if examining a rock with strange markings. When he spoke his voice was almost a whisper. 'Don't you believe in God? Aren't you afraid of what waits for you in the hereafter?'

Carrick's face took on an almost wistful expression. 'I hope there isn't a

God. If there is, then I'm headed for hell. So, I need to get everything out of this life that I can. And I can get a lot.'

'By killing people?!'

'Yes. You see, Reverend, most killers are, shall we say, vulgar people. Their speech, mannerisms and appearance are pretty crude.'

'While you are the educated gentleman.'

Carrick smiled contentedly. 'Well put. You'd be surprised how many people require a killer who doesn't look the part. There's big money to be made and I really do enjoy it. Killing is a lot more exciting than arguing a case in court.'

Lanning blurted out his deepest fear. 'Are you going to kill me?!'

'I'm afraid so.'

'But why?'

This time, the killer's laugh sounded almost pleasant. 'I don't know exactly. The person who's paying for all this wants me to become you, in order to make it easy for me to kill someone else. Of course, I can't be Reverend Jeremy

Lanning if the real Reverend Lanning is still alive. Don't take it personally, Reverend; like I said, I'm just killing you to get to someone else.'

'Who?'

Carrick maintained his pleasant demeanor. 'I honestly can't say. I'll find out when I get to Hardin.' He quickly reached down for the coffee cup. 'Now, you're going over to my horse. I have a shovel tied to my saddle.'

The pastor's voice was almost a sob as he asked a question to which he knew the answer. 'Why do I need a shovel?'

'You're going to dig your own grave, while I watch and enjoy the rest of this fine coffee.'

Reverend Lanning tried to hold back the panic that gripped him as he retrieved the shovel and began to dig. His captor's eyes never left him and he knew there was no hope in pleading for his life. Ash Carrick enjoyed killing.

The pastor shoveled steadily. His mind focused on a Buckshot Callahan dime novel, *Killers Junction*, which he had read a few months ago. Callahan had been in a situation almost exactly like this one. He had escaped by distracting his captor for a moment, then throwing the shovel at him. The shovel had landed right between the badman's eyes. The villain had dropped his gun, allowing Buckshot to jump him.

Jeremy Lanning was not a fool. He knew that a plot device in a dime novel was not likely to work in the real world. He also knew that what had worked for Callahan was the only chance he had, aside from Carrick getting struck by lightning.

Reverend Lanning looked quickly at the sky and, despite the circumstances, smiled. The Lord has blessed this area with a beautiful, sunny morning, the pastor thought to himself.

'Nice to see a man enjoying his work.' Ash took a last sip of coffee then tossed the cup to the ground. He took two steps closer to his captive, who was now standing in a fresh trench that went over his knees. 'Of course, Reverend, being a man of faith, you know that all the work a man does is to the glory of God. Correct?'

'You are an astute theologian, Carrick.'

Carrick laughed. 'That's the spirit, Pastor! After all, very shortly you will be in heaven rejoicing with the angels.'

Jeremy Lanning stopped shoveling. Now was the time. He tried to speak calmly as he quoted his dime novel hero. 'I may be parting with my life but you'll soon be parting with your scalp.'

'What do you mean?'

Lanning smirked as Callahan had done. 'Those Indians behind you don't look none too friendly.'

Carrick pivoted and looked behind him. Then he crouched and laughed as the shovel harmlessly breezed by. He lifted his pistol and, turning back to his target, fired two bullets into Jeremy Lanning. Vicious spasms jerked through the clergyman's body as he struggled to stay on his feet and then collapsed into the hole he had dug.

Carrick rose and chortled as he approached the trench. 'Nice try, Reverend, but you see, I'm a Buckshot Callahan reader myself.'

The killer looked down at the twitching body; a flow of blood created a grotesque mud at its sides. 'You got an inch or so of life left in you, Reverend. But only an inch. There's no sense in wasting another bullet on you.'

Carrick holstered his gun and picked up the shovel. 'This is going to be a pretty shallow grave, Reverend. But after the coyotes dig you up and have their feast, you will be hard to identify. By the time folks get even a glimmer of what happened to you, I will have moved on.'

A low cry of horror came from the open grave. The last sensation Jeremy Lanning experienced on earth was that of a harsh stinging as dirt began to cover his body.

7

A light tapping shattered Dehner's nightmares. His dreams were always nightmares. He opened his eyes and looked about his hotel room. He was lying fully clothed on the bed.

There was another tapping, this time a bit louder.

The last few hours came back to him. After seeing Del Burgess off, he had returned to his room and remained awake until sunup. He had then dozed for an hour or so before joining Leona and the Whitneys for breakfast. After eating, he and Leona had returned to their rooms. Leona was to pack her things and get Samuel and herself ready for the move out to the Whitneys' ranch. He had flopped on the bed to rest for just a moment . . .

'Mr Dehner?' The voice came from the other side of the door.

Rance hastily cleared his throat. He didn't want to sound drowsy. 'Yes, Leona?'

'I need to talk with you.'

'Sure. One moment.'

The detective sat up on the side of the bed, slipped socked feet into his boots, and moved quickly to the door. When he opened it, Leona was standing there cradling Samuel in her arms.

'Mr Dehner, I'm scared.'

Rance motioned her inside. 'Look, you've said yourself that you'll be as safe at the Whitney ranch as — '

'That's not what I mean.'

Dehner closed the door. 'Then, what is it?'

Leona looked down at Samuel as if checking to see that her anxiety had not spread to him. The baby was sleeping. She kissed him on the forehead before speaking in a quiet voice. 'Mr Whitney jus' came to my room. He and Mrs Whitney want me to come down to the lobby. The new preacher just came to town. They want me to meet him.'

'From what the Whitneys tell me,

Reverend Jeremy Lanning is a fine man. I'm sure you're going to — '

'Couldja come too, Mr Dehner? I know you've already done a whole heap of stuff for me, but I'm scared 'bout meetin' a preacher.'

'Why would you be scared?' Dehner felt a surge of anger directed at himself. What a fool question to ask the girl! Leona was the mother of a baby born out of wedlock. She had already been booted out of a job and a place to live by a member of the church Jeremy Lanning had come to pastor. Hardly surprising that she would feel apprehensive about meeting the clergyman.

Dehner spoke again quickly. 'Sure, I'll come. I'm looking forward to meeting the parson myself. I'm sure he's a good, kind man.'

The detective hoped he was right.

The man who awaited them in the lobby was having a cheerful conversation with Earl and Rose Whitney. There was laughter all around. The new parson watched appreciatively as Leona approached.

Dehner thought he spotted something in the clergyman's eyes that went beyond pastoral concern for a stray lamb.

Earl Whitney handled the introductions. After everyone had said hello, Ash Carrick spoke to Leona. 'I understand you and Samuel will be living with the Whitneys for a while.'

'Yes, Reverend Lannin', and I'll be safe there. You should have seen Mr Whitney yesterday. He fought three men who were rawhidin' me.'

Earl looked embarrassed. 'Yes, and if it hadn't been for Mr Dehner here, our new preacher's first duty would have been to read words at my funeral.'

There was more laughter. Dehner thought Reverend Lanning was giving him something of a quizzical look as if trying to figure out where he fitted in. It occurred to the detective that he wasn't sure where he fitted in himself.

'Mr and Mrs Whitney are both fine people,' Leona continued. 'Ask any of their ranch-hands. Why, old Hank Woodward ain't been able to do heavy work since an accident two years or so back, but they keep him on and he's not the only one, when Stu Clancy's niece got powerful sick last year they . . . '

Carrick understood that Leona was talking out of nervousness. He let her go on for a few more minutes and then posed a question in a gentle, quiet voice. 'What about you, Leona?'

'I don't follow you, Preacher.'

'You have been riding some pretty tough trails.' The fake pastor smiled with fake benevolence. 'You can't do it alone. Have you been talking with God much lately?'

The atmosphere in the lobby suddenly turned more serious and Leona turned even more nervous. 'The Whitneys tell me I should pray. I've tried some but — '

Carrick interrupted, though his voice remained soft. 'Scripture tells us, 'Words without thoughts never to heaven go.' Why don't we talk about prayer? How about tomorrow morning at ten? I'm sure Rose will be happy to look after

Samuel for you. We'll meet at the church. I would get together with you today, but I just arrived in town and I don't even know where the church is.'

A light mood returned to the lobby. Leona looked relieved.

'I'm going to introduce Jeremy to Stub Novak and some of the other deacons that are handy,' Earl explained. 'Then I'll show him the church. Why don't we all get together at Benson's Restaurant at noon? After lunch, Rose and I will take Leona and Samuel out to the ranch.'

There was the usual disconnected chatter and awkward moving about as the group slowly broke up. Rose announced that she needed to go back to her room to pick up some papers that had to be dropped off at the bank. Dehner stopped at the hotel desk before escorting Leona and Samuel back to their room.

'Are there any messages for me?' he asked.

There was a message.

★ ★ ★

Rose Whitney entered her hotel room and began to pace about. She needed to take control of her nerves. She had been involved in many underhanded dealings before. But never murder . . .

She walked to the window and pushed aside the curtains. Down the street, her husband was standing in front of Novak's General Store, joking with the owner.

The woman closed the curtains and breathed deeply as she stepped away from the window. The West was a brutal place and required hard men to tame it. Earl Whitney was strong, but Rose suspected that her husband lacked the viciousness to keep what he had built.

Rose suddenly stopped her pacing and froze. Their time was short. When was —

The door to her hotel room opened and the answer walked arrogantly in. 'Hello, Rose, can I call you Princess, just for old times' sake?'

The newcomer closed the door, grabbed Rose and kissed her passionately. The woman pressed her body against his. Her motivation wasn't desire; she needed this man right now. He was getting paid, but Rose also needed his silence. She couldn't make him angry.

The couple slowly parted. 'I've missed you, Princess.'

'I've missed you, Ash,' Rose lied.

Ash Carrick, gunfighter and killer, took a step back and admired his companion. 'I swear Rose, you're more beautiful now than when you were the headliner at the Stampede in Houston. Princess Patricia, the Pearl of Texas.'

Rose smirked. 'Before that I was Salome of the Seven Veils. I've forgotten most of the names I used.'

'The men who saw you never forgot.' Ash pulled a cigar out of the inner pocket of his coat. He bit off the end and puffed on the object as he set flame to it. 'You should be honored, Rose. I usually like my women young. Very young, about Leona's age. But I'd take you over a herd of fillies any day.'

Carrick walked over to the window and briefly parted the curtains to look outside. He gave a short, contemptuous laugh. 'Your husband thinks I've returned to my room to pray for a few minutes before meeting the church leaders of Hardin.'

'Get away from the window!' Rose snapped. 'Do you want Earl to see you?'

Ash obeyed the order and walked back toward Rose. 'You could have had a lot of rich men, Princess. Why did you settle on Whitney?'

Rose pressed her lips together before speaking. 'Earl is a good man.'

This time Carrick didn't laugh, but contempt filled his eyes. 'And good people can be manipulated, right, Princess? You're like me. You need to be the one holding the reins.'

A chill of terror ran through Rose Whitney. Could she really be like Ash Carrick? The woman promptly dismissed the notion. 'You can't stay here for long, Ash. We need to review our plans for tomorrow.'

'You mean our plans for killing poor Leona.'

Rose Whitney shivered. That chill had returned.

8

Once again, Rance Dehner lay on his hotel bed. In the room next door, Leona was singing to Samuel.

The detective reached over and took the telegram from the side table. The message was from Bertram Lowrie, his boss, the founder of the Lowrie Detective Agency. Lowrie had sent along two words in response to Dehner's earlier telegram, which explained that he would remain in Hardin to tie up loose ends. *I understand.*

Dehner placed the message back on the table. His boss did, indeed, understand. Lowrie was the only person Dehner had told about his past; a past that required him to live a certain kind of life and to strive to be a certain kind of man.

★ ★ ★

At fifteen, Rance Dehner had often been mistaken for nineteen. He was a tall kid made muscular by long hours working on the family ranch. The cattle ranch was a struggling operation that most years had less than twenty head. When it was time to take the cattle to market, Rance's father, Mitch, would sell his herd to a large ranch, the Tall K owned by Jason Kimball.

This situation troubled Rance, troubled him because his father didn't want the ranch to grow. 'We gotta stay like we is, son. We git too big, Kimball will close us down.'

'How, Pa?'

Fear crossed Mitch Dehner's face. 'He'd find a way. Powerful men like Jason Kimball, they always find them a way.'

Rance had loved his father, but he could not respect him. Inevitably, perhaps, he had developed a friendship with Buck Stevens, the sheriff of Grimsby, the town nearest his family's ranch. Buck was a large, well-built, friendly man with thick black hair and a scar on his right cheek from a time when he had been too casual in arresting a petty thief.

On Sunday mornings Rance would ride into town with his parents and two younger brothers to attend church. After the service, they would eat their one restaurant meal of the week in Grimsby. Following the meal, the rest of the family would return home. Rance would remain in town where the sheriff would teach him how to shoot, how to track and many of the other tricks 'a lawdog keeps in his bag.'

There was also plenty of talk between the lawman and his young friend. Buck would encourage the boy to read at every opportunity. 'Linda Dehner is a fine woman. Your mother taught readin' to you and your brothers. I know she prods you to pick up a book when possible. You might not always feel like it, but you do what she says.'

As he moved through his fifteenth year, Rance had become aware that Buck always spoke about Linda Dehner in very glowing terms. He knew that both his mom and Buck had spent their entire lives in the Grimsby area. Had they been sweet on each other at one time?

The question may have been at least partially answered one Sunday afternoon after Rance and Buck finished shooting old cans off a log outside of town. Buck spoke in a slightly artificial voice as he began to reload his pistol. Rance realized later that the sheriff had rehearsed this talk in his mind.

'Windy is retirin' as my deputy.'

The young man was stunned. Windy Everett had been deputy sheriff of Grimsby since Rance had been alive. 'Why?'

'Thinks he's gettin' too old for the job. Don't like to say it, but I agree. That back of his is givin' him a lot of pain.'

'What are you going to do, Sheriff?'

'Well, I've been talkin' with your mother . . . your father, too, of course. I know money is a bit tight for 'em at the ranch.'

'Yep.'

'Your younger brothers are at the age now where they can handle the heavy chores you've been doin'.'

'Reckon so.'

Buck's eyes had been darting about as he spoke. He paused for a moment then fixed his gaze on Rance. 'How'd you like to become my deputy?'

Rance was stunned. He said nothing.

The sheriff continued, 'The job pays thirty dollars a month. You'll sleep at the jailhouse most nights. You'll be able to get home one day a week and maybe sleep there — '

'Sure, Sheriff Stevens! I'd love to have the job.'

'I know you're still a few months shy of sixteen but you'll make a fine deputy, Rance. And from now on, call me Buck. We're gonna be spendin' a lot of time together.'

Rance grinned and shrugged his shoulders. I'll try not to get on your nerves, Sheriff Ste — Buck.'

The first six weeks were tough for the

new deputy sheriff. Every cowhand in the county seemed determined to test him. But Rance handled the drunken cowboys with wisdom and restraint and helped Buck Stevens to track down two outlaws who had robbed a stage. By the time he reached sixteen, Rance had gained the respect of the town of Grimsby, or at least he had the respect of what Buck called 'the decent folk'. He had also gained the affection of Beth Page. Beth worked at her family's mercantile which was located across the street from the sheriff's office. The young woman apparently made good use of the store's large window. She seemed to always make it over to the sheriff's office when Buck Stevens was gone and Rance was there by himself.

Rance pretended to be irritated by the visits. But the pretending became increasingly hard to keep up. At fourteen, or fourteen and a half as she insisted on giving her age, Beth stood at a little over five feet with hair the color of fresh straw, angelic blue eyes, and a smile with just a touch of the devil.

On a Monday morning, Rance glanced frequently out the window of the sheriff's office after Buck Stevens left to do a round. When he spotted Beth crossing the street, he hurried behind the desk and pretended to be reading circulars.

'Sitting behind a desk, that's all you're good for, Rance Dehner! What'd happen if you had to do real work?' The girl smirked playfully as she closed the door behind her.

'Well, good morning to you, Miss Page.' Rance stood up from the desk.

'What are you gonna do now?'

'What do you mean?'

'Are you going to do something useful or what?'

'Well . . . I did have something on my mind. Nothing too important, mind you.'

Beth giggled. 'I don't think you ever get anything important on that mind of yours.'

Rance began to fumble his words as he stepped away from the desk. 'The reason I'm leaving the desk is because what I have to say is not official. This has nothing to do with me being a deputy sheriff.'

'Oh.'

'Have you heard about the dance this Saturday night?'

'Yes . . . I've heard,' the girl replied.

'I was wondering if maybe you'd like to go.'

'You mean go with you?'

'Ah . . . yes.'

'Guess so. But I'll be wearing heavy boots. You're so clumsy, Rance Dehner, you'll probably step on my feet a thousand times.'

'Well, if that don't . . . When folks ask me why I brought you to the dance, I'll just tell them the truth: that you were the gal who was closest by. I didn't even have to cross the street to ask you!'

There was a moment of silence as both Rance and Beth studied the floor. Beth was first to speak. 'Sorry, 'bout what I just said. Don't know why I spoke like that. Truth is, I've been hoping you'd ask me.'

'There's no reason to be sorry. I've been wanting to ask, but was nervous about it.'

'Why?' Beth's voice was now completely sincere. 'You shoulda known I'd say yes.'

The two young people looked directly at each other and something very special passed between them. They both laughed for no particular reason and then came together in a hug. They parted reluctantly, Beth turning her head to glance across the street.

'I have to get back. Pa already complains I spend too much time over here.'

'Buck will be returning from his round pretty soon.'

Beth giggled and that devilish smile played across her face. 'I know that. I know when Sheriff Stevens does his rounds and you are all by your lonesome here in the office.'

The girl gave Rance a fast kiss on the cheek, then turned and ran out of the office almost colliding with the sheriff.

'Good morning, Sheriff Stevens!' Her

voice was a joyous shout.

'Good morning, Beth.' Buck Stevens slowly stepped into the office as he watched the young woman run across the street. 'I don't think I've ever seen anybody look so happy without a drink or two in them.'

The sheriff turned and faced his deputy. 'You're lookin' mighty pleased yourself.'

Three days later Beth Page was spending even more time in the sheriff's office. Buck Stevens was at Clem Myer's ranch investigating a case of cattle rustling. Beth paced about the office jubilantly while Rance cleaned one of the rifles that lined a wall in the office.

'There's something I can't tell you,' the girl said in a teasing manner.

'OK.' Rance didn't look up from the Henry. Beth wasn't the only one who could tease. Rance knew Beth was no good at keeping secrets.

'Ma says it would be bad luck to tell you.'

'Better listen to your ma.'

'Well . . . I'm making a new dress for the dance! Ma is helping me. It's gonna be beautiful. We've got — '

The door to the office banged open. Willy, an elderly man who swamped out the town's largest saloon, hobbled in. 'Gotta see Buck.'

'He's out of town. What can I do for you, Willy?'

Willy looked a bit confused, as if uncertain as to whether Rance was up to the job. But his hesitation was brief. 'Jared Kimball just pistol-whipped one of the whor — ' He stopped, looked at Beth then continued. 'One of the gals at the Quick Dollar saloon.'

'Why?' Rance sprang up from the desk and quickly returned the Henry to the rack.

'No reason,' Willy answered. 'You know how Jared gets when he's had a few drinks. Meaner than a hungry wolf. He's braggin' 'bout shootin' the place up, then takin' over the town. Reckon he knows Buck's gone.'

'Thanks, Willy.' Rance quickly checked

his pistol. 'I'll get right over there.'

'Wait for Sheriff Stevens to get back!' Beth shouted. 'The two of you can handle it together.'

Rance's reply was abrupt. 'Can't wait. Don't know when Buck is getting back.'

The young woman's voice became pleading. 'Jared Kimball thinks he can do what he wants, because his pa owns the biggest ranch.'

'I know.' Rance started for the door.

Beth took after him. 'Jared hates you; he thinks it's wrong for you to be a deputy sheriff, because your people are . . . well . . . they own a small ranch, not like the Tall K.'

'Girl's right!' Willy said. 'And Jared came to town with two or more hands from the ranch. Those men won't let nothin' happen to Jared. You stay away, boy! Wait till — '

Rance paused by the door and spoke loudly. 'Wait until Jared Kimball pistol-whips someone else or maybe kills somebody?' Beth was a bit stunned. It was the first time she had heard him raise his voice in genuine anger.

Rance took a deep breath. Jared would be hoorawing him. He had to keep his emotions in check. 'Willy, could you stay here and sit at the desk? Tell anyone who comes in I'll be back soon.'

'Sure.'

'Thanks.' He took Beth by one arm and walked her out of the office.

Standing with her on the boardwalk, Rance could see the moisture forming in her eyes. 'You get back to work, Beth. Soon as this is over, I'll come by the store. OK?'

Beth nodded her head. Rance left her there.

As he approached, he saw Doc Petterson and two other men carrying a woman out of the Quick Dollar. He caught up with them in the middle of the street. 'Is she going to be all right, Doctor?'

'Think so. She's been beaten bad. We're getting her to my office now.'

Rance glanced at the victim. What he

saw inflamed a deep anger inside him.

Walking toward the batwing doors of the Quick Dollar, he remembered what Buck Stevens had advised him. *When you are walkin' into a dangerous situation, check it out. Makes no difference how many times you've seen a place before, look at it careful like if you can.*

Dehner stopped in front of the town's largest drinking hole. He noted that the Quick Dollar looked like a typical western saloon. The second floor was horseshoe-shaped with plenty of rooms where commerce was conducted. The stairway on one side of the saloon was wide, allowing for a lot of traffic. The banister, which ran up the stairway and across the second floor, was strong and ornate.

Jared Kimball was leaning against the center of the bar holding court. Beside him were two hands from the Tall K: Gus and Billy. Both men were in their early twenties and bragged about being fast with their guns. Their claims had gone untested.

Rance remembered that Jared was usually accompanied by three men. The third was an older guy who called himself Fargo. Buck didn't like Fargo, a man who instigated gunfights with greenhorns he knew he could outdraw. But, so far, the sheriff hadn't been able to take any legal action against the man. 'That jasper always goads the other guy to go for his gun first.'

The saloon was crowded and noisy with people escaping the afternoon heat. No one noticed Rance as he entered. Despite the bright sun outside, the saloon was dark and several kerosene lamps had been lit. It always seems to be night in the Quick Dollar, Rance thought.

Somewhere in the chaos a piano player with little talent pounded a contraption that had probably never been tuned. Near the stairway on the right, several saloon girls were busy encouraging a passel of male fools who were losing money at the roulette table.

The deputy walked across the Quick Dollar and approached the bar from the left side of the saloon. It was less crowded. Jared Kimball saw him coming. 'Well, well, Deputy Rance Dehner. How are you enjoyin' all that big money you're makin'?'

Dehner said nothing. Kimball guffawed and kept talking. 'Yep, Dehner here is pullin' in thirty dollars a month. That's more than he made in a year at that little ten-cow outfit his family's got.'

Jared Kimball was tall and lanky with hair the color of a starless night. He had an oval-shaped face, which seemed to hold a constant sneer.

'You're under arrest, Jared.' Dehner spoke in a monotone.

Kimball responded with a loud laugh. 'What for?'

'Assault.'

'You talkin' about Abby, that red-headed dove?' Jared continued to lean his back against the bar. Gus and Billy remained one on each side of him but they took a step away from the bright mahogany. Their hands hovered over their guns.

'Right now, Abby's hair is red with blood. I'm taking you to jail.'

'We'll just see about that.' Kimball walked away from the bar with a fake casualness. He stopped near the center of the saloon, pushed back a vacant table then faced the deputy directly. 'You know why I hate you so much, Dehner?'

Rance took a couple of steps, which placed him directly opposite to Kimball and about six yards away. The crowd parted, but not in the usual manner. There was snickering and an almost gleeful sense of anticipation. Three guns against one, a deputy sheriff was about to get shot down. Something to talk about tomorrow.

Jared's question had surprised Dehner but he was grateful for the opening. 'Now, let me think that question over.' The deputy twisted his face in a mockingly thoughtful manner as he skimmed the crowd for someone else who might decide to assist Jared Kimball. For a moment his eyes hit the batwing doors.

Beth was standing outside watching the events unfold. He checked his anxiety and continued his sweep of the saloon.

On the second floor, a man and a woman stepped out of one of the rooms, laughing. The laughter stopped as the man looked down. He pushed the woman back into the room and followed her. A speck of light winked from the room as the man drew his gun. Rance had recognized him as Fargo.

Dehner smiled as he answered Kimball's question in a slow, friendly voice. 'Well ... golly ... I can't imagine why you don't like me, Jared. Maybe it's because I'm a Baptist and you're a Methodist.'

'Not hardly. It's because you got an itch inside you 'bout right and wrong. You got that itch because you come from trash. Poor people always hang on to religion and other hogwash. Your family's ranch is a joke. If my father didn't buy those scarecrows your old man calls cattle, you'd have starved years ago. But don't worry, Dehner, I'm gonna put an end to your misery today.'

That would have been an obvious moment for Jared to go for his gun, but the wealthy rancher's son was too smart for that. The saloon was now completely quiet except for the still spinning roulette wheel, which made a sound like an angry swarm of insects. Kimball's body appeared loose, but his eyes were fixed on Dehner. 'Tell me, Mr Deputy Sheriff, do you know the real reason you got your job?'

'What do you mean?'

'My father has lived in these parts all his life. It seems your ma and Buck Stevens usta be friends. Real — good — friends.'

Kimball's face took on a look of cruel mockery but Dehner saw the man's chest rise as he did a slight inhale. Jared's gun had just cleared leather when a bullet from Rance's Colt slammed into his shoulder and pushed him backward. Kimball's pistol fired into a wall just before he stumbled and fell.

As he pulled the trigger, Rance

jumped sideways. He hit the floor as the gunslick from the second-story room ran to the railing and fired a bullet that burrowed into one of the gambling tables. Rance snapped off two shots toward the second floor. Both bullets hit their target. Fargo dropped his weapon. His body went into spasms as he plunged over the railing.

Red heat passed over Dehner's head. He rolled toward the batwings, then, lying on his stomach took a quick look in the direction of the bar. Gus had a smoking revolver in hand. Billy looked dazed. He held a gun but it was pointed at the floor.

As Gus raised his arm for another shot, Dehner sent a bullet into his chest. Gus staggered, fired two shots, and fell to the ground.

Screams, shouting and chaos filled the Quick Dollar as Dehner slowly got to his feet. From what he could tell, Fargo and Gus were dead. Billy had holstered his gun. He still looked dazed.

A couple of barflies were helping

Jared Kimball to his feet. Rance laughed in a caustic manner. Two men were killed trying to save Kimball from a fight he had provoked. But Jared would only suffer a wound, which would heal in a few months.

Rance suddenly realized that Buck Stevens was standing beside him. Buck yelled at the bartender. 'Len, get Doc Petterson.'

'Doc is busy patching up — '

'Get the doctor now!'

'Yes, Sheriff!' Len ran from behind the bar.

At first, Rance couldn't understand Buck's orders. Then he heard a soft, feminine voice behind him. 'Take it easy, honey. Doc will be here soon.'

Rance turned and saw one of the saloon girls, Cindy, crouched over Beth Page. He froze for a moment, refusing to accept what was in front of him. Beth was lying on the floor, blood seemed to cover her entire body.

He crouched beside Beth; the girl's eyes were closed and her face twisted by pain. He looked across Beth at Cindy, who was holding a towel on one of the girl's wounds. The saloon girl spoke frantically, 'I can't seem to stop the bleeding . . . '

Rance's voice sounded like a desperate cry. 'Doc will be here soon, he's got to be.'

Beth's eyes opened. 'Rance?'

'I'm right here, Beth.'

'Are you OK?'

'Yes, I'm fine.'

A slight smile fought against the girl's pain. 'I saw you fall. Thought you'd been shot . . . '

Cindy spoke in a low, reverent whisper. 'She came running through the doors to help you. Took those last two bullets Gus fired.'

Rance took Beth's hand in his. The girl's smile brightened, her weak voice became steadier. 'We're still going to the dance this Saturday.'

'We sure are.'

'Tonight Ma and me are workin' on the dress. It's going to look so nice . . . '

Beth's voice stopped. For a moment Rance continued to talk to her about the dance. Words flooded out of his mouth in a senseless, tormented barrage. His voice became more frantic, his mind refusing to accept the obscene tragedy in front of him.

Doctor Petterson came running through the batwing doors. Cindy stood up and the doctor took her place. He felt the girl's wrist as he looked at her wounds.

'Oh, no,' he said. 'Dear God, no.'

Rance Dehner could say nothing.

He remained in town for another three months. Buck Stevens tried to console him, but it didn't work. The wide window in the mercantile across the street from the sheriff's office now stood as a condemnation, a constant reminder of how one act of selfishness had cost the life of a young woman he loved.

Two years in the army got him away from Grimsby and helped him to hone the skills Buck Stevens had taught him. After leaving the military, he became a Pinkerton operative. He was assigned to the office in Dallas. While there he heard some of his colleagues joking about a 'crazy limey' who was opening up a detective agency to compete with Pinkerton.

Dehner went to see the crazy limey.

Bertram Lowrie stood well over six feet, thin almost to the point of appearing emaciated. He had iron-gray hair and the bearing of a man who had spent many years in the British military.

Lowrie stared at the young man who sat in the hard wooden chair in front of his desk. 'Your reputation precedes you, Mr Dehner,' he said in a crisp manner. 'You have been with Pinkerton for little more than a year and have already solved a major case for them. So why leave?'

Dehner stared into the stern, hawk-like face and realized that anything short of the truth would not do. He also realized that Bertram Lowrie was a man who could be trusted with the truth. 'I want to be a detective, sir. But not a Pinkerton. I don't want to work strikes or what they call domestic cases.'

'I agree,' Lowrie replied. 'Allan J. Pinkerton is quite enthused about getting his company involved in labor disputes. That is his decision. The money is good, I'm sure. But this agency will not perform that kind of service ... or trail after unfaithful spouses.' Lowrie leaned back in his chair, but the intensity of his stare did not diminish. 'Tell me about your experiences as a deputy.'

After more than three years, Dehner talked about that horrible day, the day in which he caused the death of an innocent young woman.

'I don't understand, Mr Dehner. The death of Beth Page was a terrible tragedy. But it was an accident. There was nothing you could have done.'

'You're wrong, sir. I saw Beth standing at the doors of the saloon. I knew immediately what I needed to do. I should have left the saloon and walked the girl back to the mercantile. I should have told her parents to keep her there.

But I didn't do that . . . '

Dehner couldn't continue but he didn't need to, Bertram Lowrie understood. 'You were afraid of losing face,' Lowrie said. 'You were sixteen and felt that if you left the saloon in the midst of a stand-off, people would laugh at you.'

Dehner sat erect in his chair. A ferocious anger seemed to grip his body. 'Because of my damned pride, a wonderful woman was savagely slaughtered. She ran into that saloon because she thought I had been hurt.'

Dehner began to breathe heavily. Drops of perspiration made paths down his forehead. He closed his eyes for a moment, calming the tumult inside of him. He opened his eyes, and spoke in a toneless manner. 'I will carry the memory of how I failed Beth Page to my grave. I want to be a detective who helps people. I can never make up for what I have done. But that's no reason not to try.'

Lowrie nodded his head. 'Do you

visit Grimsby much?'

'No. My parents are both dead. Natural causes. My brothers run the ranch. It's growing. The Kimballs leave them alone.'

'And Sheriff Stevens?'

'He's gone, too,' Dehner answered. 'But not from natural causes. Some barfly shot him in the back one night while he was doing a round. I never asked Buck about ... about his friendship with my mother.'

There were several moments of silence, then Bertram Lowrie spoke. 'I've learned enough, Mr Dehner. When can you start work?'

★ ★ ★

Sounds of *The Battle Hymn of the Republic* came from the next room. The song sounded a bit strange being sung as a lullaby in Leona's soft voice. Dehner wasn't worried about the young woman or her baby at this moment; they were safe for the time being. But they would need him later. He had to grab some sleep while he could.

He dozed off as Leona sang, '*Let the hero, born of woman, crush the serpent with his heel . . .*'

9

Ash Carrick checked his timepiece and then smiled as he looked about the church. Leona was due for their meeting in about ten minutes. Her life would be over in less than an hour.

The church was in a good location, a short walk outside of town. At ten o'clock on a weekday morning, no one would be passing by.

Carrick recalled the conversation he had had the previous day with Rose Whitney in her hotel room. 'Kill Leona. Make it quick and quiet.' Rose spoke in a low, intense whisper; she wasn't enjoying this. 'Then take her body far away and bury it. You are never to be seen in this town again.'

'Aren't you going to miss me, Rose?'

Rose Whitney ignored the question. 'People will think Reverend Jeremy Lanning violated Leona, then ran off with her. You are being well paid, Ash. Staying away from Hardin is not asking much. Besides this one job, there is nothing here for you.'

Rose flinched but only briefly. She had just revealed her true feelings about Ash Carrick. A new hardness came into the woman's eyes as she stared at the killer for hire.

Carrick smirked, and casually fussed with his cigar. 'I talked with Jeremy Lanning a spell before killing him. He was a real reverend, not just someone who preaches in a medicine show. I'd guess the man has friends. People who will look into — '

'Yes, yes.' The woman waved her hand as if dismissing the matter. 'Reverend Lanning will eventually be exonerated. The law will find out that an imposter killed the pastor and probably killed Leona. That won't affect my plans.'

Carrick's eyebrows went up. 'What exactly are your plans?'

'You needn't concern yourself with that.'

The killer slowly inhaled on his stogie and then loosed a cloud of smoke. 'Who are you working with, Rose?'

'What do you mean?'

'There's a lot going on here you haven't told me.'

The woman replied in a low mumble. 'There is a lot going on here that you don't need to know.' Rose walked over to the chest of drawers and reached into the handbag she had placed there. She pulled out an envelope and handed it to Carrick. 'I am paying you in full, in advance. I'm trusting you to perform the job well. Goodbye, Ash. We won't be seeing each other again.'

Ash took a few hasty steps toward the woman. 'How about — '

She held out the envelope. 'Goodbye, Ash.'

Ash Carrick sat in the front pew of the church and looked the place over. The killer mused to himself that he hadn't spent much time in churches but this one resembled the few he had been inside. There were ten pews on each side of a wide aisle that ran down the middle of the church. The platform in front contained a pulpit and a choir loft immediately behind it.

He examined the church's carpet. It was surprisingly thick and well cared for. A perfect place for . . . he recalled Rose's words, 'People will think Reverend Lanning violated Leona . . . ' The killer laughed whimsically. 'Violated.' Rose made rape sound as if it were a disregard of a town ordinance. But Rose was, by her own choosing, out of his life forever. Yes indeed, Leona would be violated.

One of the double doors that fronted the church opened slowly. A girlish voice followed the creaks. 'Reverend Lanning? Are you here?'

Carrick bounded to his feet and stepped quickly up the aisle. 'Leona, it's good to see you. How did your first night at the Whitney ranch go?'

'Jus' fine.' Leona stepped inside and carefully closed the door behind her. 'Mrs Whitney's been very nice to me.

Last night we read the Good Book together.' She nodded downward at the Bible in her right hand.

'That's wonderful.'

'We read Matthew chapter six; that should help our talk, right Reverend?'

'Well . . . ah . . . '

'That chapter says a lot 'bout prayer. Ain't that whatcha wanna talk to me 'bout?'

'Of course!' He placed an arm around Leona. 'Let's have our little talk in the front pew. It's a bit more comfortable.'

As they walked toward the front of the church, Carrick tightened his arm around Leona.

'Reverend Lanning, I'd 'preciate it if you'd take your arm off me.'

'My, my, aren't you the prim and proper lady!' Carrick ripped the top part of Leona's dress and pushed her to the floor in front of the first pew. The Bible flew from her hand, hit the armrest on the side of the pew, and then hit the floor. Carrick crouched over her, grabbing both of her arms.

'Let me go! I'll — '

'You'll do what I say!'

Carrick didn't hear the footsteps until it was too late. He stood up in time to take a blow to the middle of his face. He plunged against the edge of the church's platform, yelling in pain.

Dehner grabbed the lapels of Carrick's frock coat, lifted him up and delivered another hard punch, this time to the fake pastor's left eye. Dehner's left hand remained on the coat, propping Carrick up and allowing the detective to deliver another blow, this one a haymaker that spun Carrick and dropped him to the floor.

The killer lay on his back. He gave a low moan, gently placed a hand on his face, and then withdrew it. 'My nose . . . broken . . . '

'I'm just getting started,' Dehner shouted in an angry voice.

'Let's end his miserable life right now!'

Carrick looked up. What he saw was

not encouraging. Rance Dehner stood on one side of him, fists clenched; at Carrick's feet stood Deputy Max Chumley. The lawman held a .45 in his hand.

Chumley cocked the revolver. 'We don't cotton much to men who beat women.'

Carrick's voice sputtered words of desperation. 'Leona fell, I was just trying — '

Dehner placed a boot on Carrick's windpipe and pressed downwards. 'No more lies, understand?'

He lifted the boot allowing Carrick to wheeze out, 'Understand.'

The boot remained on the outlaw's throat, though Dehner did not press down as he spoke. 'What is your real name?'

'Ash Carrick.'

'Wowee! Mr Ash Carrick!' Chumely's voice boomed with something between boyish enthusiasm and madness. 'We got us a circular on this fella. Seems he's wanted for murder in Houston, or is it Dallas? Looks like you've shaved that beard the circular said you had, Mr Carrick. Don't make no never mind. Think maybe I'll save everyone a lot of trouble — '

Carrick held up a trembling hand. 'No, no, please . . . '

Dehner laughed inwardly. Max Chumley was playing his part well. Now it was his turn. 'I want you to talk, Carrick. And like I said, no more lies.'

'Yes, sure.'

'What happened to the real Reverend Lanning?'

Ash Carrick began to collect himself. He was no fool. The killer realized his situation was desperate. His only hope was to escape from prison. He also knew that Rose Whitney had a way of getting things done. Just maybe . . .

'I asked you a question, Carrick!' Dehner yelled. 'What happened to Reverend Lanning!'

'I killed him,' Lanning answered. 'His body is buried about a two-hour ride northeast, near a grove of cottonwoods.

I can draw you a map.'

The detective was pleased to get that information but, of course, it cost the killer nothing to reveal it. Carrick was already wanted for another murder. Keeping a boot on the killer's neck, Dehner moved to his next question.

'Why did you kill the pastor?'

'To get to Leona Carson. She was the target.'

'Why kill Leona?'

'I don't know. It was a business deal. A contract.'

Dehner's voice became more intense. 'Who paid you?'

Carrick had anticipated the question and grabbed at the only lie he could concoct. 'I was paid by a go-between in San Antonio, a specialist in setting up such arrangements.'

'His name?'

'He used a phony name, Joe Collins. For his next client he was probably Bill Jones.'

Dehner wasn't sure Ash Carrick was telling the truth. The detective did notice that the killer's face was becoming increasingly pale as blood flowed from his nose. He'd be unconscious soon if something wasn't done quickly.

'Hold your sleeve against your nose, Carrick.' There was no sympathy in the detective's voice. He glanced toward Max Chumley. 'Help me lift this skunk.'

Max holstered his gun. 'Sure. I guess it is getting time to put out the garbage.'

As the two men lifted Carrick to his feet, the deputy gave Leona a concerned look. 'Are you all right, Miss Carson?'

Leona was standing a few feet up the aisle. One hand was pressed against her shoulder. 'Yes, I'm fine. I jus' havta hold my dress in place where it got tore — '

Chumley's face went red. 'Sure, I understand.'

'Thanks for helping, Leona,' Dehner said as he and Max began to walk the killer toward the front door. Leona stepped between two pews to make room for the strange procession.

'Take that dress to a seamstress,' Dehner said as the threesome passed by the girl. 'We'll pay to have it fixed. It would be a shame to lose such a nice dress.'

Max Chumley smiled broadly. 'Yep, it sure is a mighty pretty dress.'

Leona returned the smile. She began to follow the men up the aisle and then hastily turned and began to walk back.

'Anything wrong?' the deputy asked.

'I can't forget the Good Book.' Still holding the dress in place, Leona returned to the front of the church and scooped up her Bible.

10

Ash Carrick sat on a cot in his jail cell and glared at the three men who fronted him in a half circle. 'You morons have nothing better to do than watch a man bleed to death?' The killer's frock coat was lying on the floor of his cell, the right sleeve blotted with red. Carrick now pressed a handkerchief against his nose. Despite the circumstances, Dehner was a tad amused. The handkerchief, provided by Sheriff Amos Santell, looked none too clean.

Dehner stood in the middle of the half circle; Sheriff Santell on one side and his deputy on the other. 'I'd be careful who I called a moron,' Dehner said in a cheerful manner. 'You've been acting pretty stupid yourself.'

The reply came in a nasal twang. 'What do you mean?'

'Yesterday, you quoted the Bible, 'Words

without thoughts never to heaven go.'
Only that's not from the Bible, Carrick.
You were quoting Shakespeare — *Hamlet*.'

'I knew that! I didn't think a bunch
of small-town bumpkins would.'

Dehner continued, 'It didn't impress
me as the kind of mistake a pastor
would make. This morning, I enlisted
Deputy Chumley. We stopped Leona
when she got to town for her
appointment. I gave her that line about
Matthew, chapter six. Max and I were
standing right outside the church door
when she delivered it. Your response
was very uncertain. That's when Max
and I hurried in and hid behind a back
pew.'

'Are you some religious fanatic,
Dehner?' Carrick tried to sound tough
but couldn't bring it off.

There was a touch of melancholy in
Dehner's reply. 'I'm just a man who has
a lot of time to read.'

Max Chumley was not one bit
melancholy. 'Maybe you should start

reading the Good Book, Carrick, in what little time you got left.'

'Why don't you use some of your time to get a doctor over here?'

Carrick glanced at the sheriff's handkerchief, which was getting increasingly red.

'Doc will be around when he gets to it!' Amos Santell declared angrily. 'He's got decent folk to patch up 'fore he's gotta waste time on you!'

The sheriff's anger was genuine but not aimed altogether at the killer. Santell was a bit miffed because Dehner had used Max Chumley instead of him to trap the killer. Amos had been relegated to fetching the doctor.

'Does this stinking hole of a town have a lawyer?' Carrick's question was calculated, but his interrogators didn't realize it.

'We got one, name of John Latchman,' Chumley answered.

'I want to see him!' Carrick came as close to shouting as he could. He planned to use the lawyer as a go between. He needed to get in touch with Rose Whitney. Rose knew men who could bust open any jail. And he knew enough about Rose to send her to prison. She would do as he ordered.

'I'll stop by Latchman's office on my next round,' Chumley replied.

'I think we should leave Mr Carrick by himself for a while,' Dehner said. 'He's getting a little too used to making demands.'

Dehner and his two companions sauntered out of the jail cell. Sheriff Santell closed the jail door loudly behind him and smiled at the prisoner as he turned the key in the lock. The three men didn't look back as they walked from the jail area into the office.

Dehner pushed back his flat-crowned hat and scratched his head. 'I have a favor to ask, Sheriff.'

'What might that be?' Amos was still a bit irked with the detective.

'Could you deputize me? I'll be a volunteer, of course.'

'What for?'

Dehner suddenly became aware of the sheriff's anger. He immediately understood why. His involving Deputy Chumley in his plans had made sense from a stand point of strategy but it was bad politics.

He replied in a toneless voice. 'You have a known killer in your jail. That's going to put more responsibility on — '

'There's more to it than that!' Santell shot back.

The detective's voice remained a mono-tone. 'You're absolutely right. I'm staying in Hardin until we find out who's trying to kill Leona. If I'm a deputy, more doors will be open to me.' Dehner smiled and shrugged his shoulders. 'Besides, I might as well make myself a bit useful.'

Amos smirked, opened a desk drawer and tossed a badge at Dehner. 'Whatcha gonna do first to make yourself useful?'

Dehner caught the tin star with one hand. 'I'm going over to Mrs Conklin's place — the seamstress. Leona is over there getting her dress fixed. I'll ride with the girl to the Whitney ranch. I think she's still a bit shaken. When I get back, I will be at your service, Sheriff.'

Max Chumley watched Dehner leave the office and then spoke up immediately. 'Guess I'd better do a round.'

'Yeah, I guess you'd better.'

After Max left the office, Amos Santell went to the window and watched his deputy. He was heading for the newspaper office.

The sheriff sighed and ran a hand through his hair. He knew he should be happy to have Dehner as a volunteer deputy. He needed all the help he could get. All this stuff about someone trying to kill Leona Carson was just crazy.

He walked back to his desk and sat down. Yes, that was it. That is what really made him mad about this whole mess: the craziness. Phony preachers quoting Shakespeare instead of the Bible . . .

Santell picked up some circulars and began to thumb through them. He wanted to go back to being a small-town sheriff, back to handling barflies and owlhoots who couldn't spell Shakespeare, never mind quote him.

The lawman tossed the circulars on to the desk and reached for his tobacco pouch. 'It's gonna be a while 'fore that happens,' he said out loud.

11

John Latchman lifted the window shade in his small office. The citizens of Hardin appeared to be about their usual, boring business. The lawyer thought about the future and how different the town would look in only a couple of years. Some of the folks walking by his window right now wouldn't survive. He'd do a lot more than survive.

Latchman's thoughts suddenly took a different direction. Rose Whitney was crossing the street to his office. Egad, the woman looked beautiful! How did she do it? Rose always managed to dress in a way that wouldn't arouse the ire of the church folks but still made a man feel . . .

John Latchman opened the door of his office. 'Good morning, Mrs Whitney.'

'Good morning, Mr Latchman.' Rose stood in the doorway, her voice polite and proper. 'It appears that I am your first client for the day.'

'Indeed, I have no appointments for the next hour, please come in.' Latchman motioned her inside with a grand sweep of his right arm.

As Rose entered the office, she handed the lawyer a large brown envelope. 'Camouflage,' she said.

John looked amused as he closed the door. 'What do you mean?'

'The papers inside that envelope are not important but I want you to scatter them on the front of your desk. People passing by who glance inside will think we are discussing legal matters regarding the ranch.'

John's eyes gave his visitor an appreciative once over. 'I just opened that window shade; it would be no trouble at all to close it again.'

Rose smiled in an overly demure manner. 'Not this morning, Mr Latchman.'

Latchman's demeanor turned serious. 'Rose, I can't be satisfied with our occasional moments together, I have to — '

'I feel the same way,' the woman replied quickly. 'But there are some very serious matters we have to discuss and I don't have much time. Earl expects me home by lunch.'

John gave Rose another appreciative once over. 'Well then, I guess we had better get down to business.' He walked around his desk and began to spread the papers Rose had brought on to it. 'I got a letter yesterday from Dallas. That spur line the railroad is going to build through Hardin should be here in less than six months. This town is going to explode, Rose, and you and I will own it.'

Rose smiled at the lawyer and noted, not for the first time, that John Latchman was a remarkably handsome man. He stood at slightly less than six feet and was well built. His brown hair and pencil mustache were given fastidious care; the man was vain. His expensive, perfectly tailored suit confirmed that fact. But John covered his vanity with a polite old-world charm, which also disguised his ambition. John Latchman was a man who would go far.

And he was madly in love with her. Rose took a very special pride in that. She was at least five years older than he was. The town's young single women were always batting their eyes at the handsome lawyer but he paid them no mind. Rose Whitney owned John Latchman and that fact gave her a sense of power.

Both the lawyer and his client sat down and exchanged a laugh; the laughter of two people who shared a secret. John playfully employed a formal tone. 'Now, what can I do for you this morning, Mrs Whitney?'

Rose paused before speaking. This wasn't going to be easy. 'Do you know about Ash Carrick, the killer they have in jail?'

John gave her a whimsical smirk. 'How could I not know? This town is talking about nothing else. It seems that the Hardin Methodist Church is going to have to find a new pastor. I hope the next chap doesn't encounter a killer on his way here to do the Lord's work.'

Rose spoke without emotion. 'Ash Carrick must be killed.'

Latchman shrugged his shoulders. 'No doubt he will be. The man is already wanted for one murder and — '

'I mean he must be killed today.'

John Latchman looked startled. It was an expression Rose had never seen on the lawyer's face before. Methodically, she explained why Carrick had to die and who was financing the efforts to murder Leona Carson. She left out only the details of her past relationship with Carrick.

Latchman's expression went from being startled to being overwhelmed. 'So, Carrick can implicate you in the murder of the preacher.'

'Yes.'

The lawyer's voice didn't waver. 'Then, you are right, we must kill him. Today.'

Rose continued in her matter-of-fact manner. 'It should be easy to pull off. Sheriff Santell is just a small-town sheriff, nothing more. Max Chumley is smarter than his boss but still a green kid. There is only one person I fear.'

'Who's that?'

'Rance Dehner. Dehner brought Leona back to the ranch yesterday. I found out that he's going to serve as a volunteer deputy. He's determined to catch the person who is trying to kill Leona.'

Latchman looked troubled. 'Why? What's it to him? I've heard all the barroom chatter about Dehner. He works for the Lowrie Detective agency. He tracked a hired killer, Curt Tatum, to this area and killed him. That ended his assignment. Nobody is paying Dehner to protect Leona Carson. Why is he still here?'

A worried expression clouded Rose's face. She began to work her hands. 'He will only say that he is a detective and doesn't like unanswered questions. Dehner scares me. I don't understand him. And he's driven. Men like that are dangerous.' Rose was determined to stop Dehner but she said nothing about that to her lover.

'I agree we've got to . . . ' Latchman

stared out the window. 'Well, well, it looks like we might be in luck.'

Rose turned her head. Through the window, she saw Max Chumley standing outside of Fredrickson's Hardware Store talking with the owner. Rose and Latchman exchanged knowing smiles. Rose headed for the door and opened it as across the street, Ralph Fredrickson was sauntering back into his store.

'Max Chumley, you get over here right away!' The woman waved as she shouted.

When the deputy entered the lawyer's office he found two people beaming bright smiles at him. 'Deputy, I want to apologize for the way I behaved yesterday.' John's smile turned warm and friendly. 'Mrs Whitney, yesterday our town's deputy stopped by my office and asked if I'd see Ash Carrick. My mind was so tied up with legal mumbo-jumbo that I brushed him off. As I recall, I was downright rude.'

'Mr Latchman! You should be ashamed of yourself. Why, Max Chumley is the hero of Hardin, Texas.'

The adoring look of a beautiful woman caused Max's face to turn red. He glanced downward. 'That's OK, Mr Latchman. You were right busy at the time.'

'Are you on a round right now, Mr Chumley?' Rose asked.

'Sort of, I reckon. I just came from the newspaper office. Rod Baker called in the photographer fella to have my picture took. Rod's gonna stop by the sheriff's office this afternoon and get the whole story. It will run in Saturday's edition. Rod is sure that it will also run in the big city papers.'

'Well, I can't wait for Saturday's edition!' Rose proclaimed.

'Neither can I!' John pointed at one of the two chairs in front of his desk. 'Please sit down, Deputy.'

'Yes,' Rose spoke in a girlish, eager manner. 'We want to hear about everything that happened yesterday and what you have planned for today.'

Max hesitated, but only for a moment. 'I guess I do got a few minutes to spare.'

12

June sat in the Lucky Lady saloon, absent-mindedly running a finger in the moisture on the table in front of her. A well-dressed gent strutted down the wide stairway perched in the middle of the saloon. He walked by her as if she didn't exist. The woman frowned and continued with her art work. Men were such fools, she thought, most women too, for that matter.

June hated the town of Hardin and hated her life. She hated having to make drunken cowboys and worthless saddletramps happy. Riding herd on the other girls was no joy, either. She had been promised some extra money to 'keep the doves clean in their cages,' as the boss had put it. So far, she hadn't seen any of that lucre.

The woman stared at the table where she had written 'June Day', the name everyone called her. She used to think it was funny. But that was a long time ago.

Her real name was June Preston. She had been married to Harold Preston for about a year. They were the owners of Preston's Mercantile in a dusty town that now seemed a million miles away. Harold had taken the store over when his father died. They were doing well, but she was twenty and bored. Life seemed so routine and limited.

The woman laughed bitterly. She had been gullible . . . and stupid. A handsome gambler had come into the store one cool morning and joked about her name, calling her 'June Day.' Within a week, he was painting beautiful verbal pictures of a life full of riches and splendor.

June wiped her name from the table and, as she often did, thought about Harold Preston. How had he reacted when he read her note? Did he still run the store? Did he find another wife?

The woman's eyes shifted to the left

and she glanced at her reflection in the mirror behind the bar. Her make-up had been applied hastily and it showed. Her brown hair looked uncombed. But, despite all the obvious indifference, she still looked pretty. However, with the life she was leading, how much longer would that last?

June's eyes shifted and she glanced over at the batwings. It was late afternoon. She felt tired. June Day was twenty-three and always seemed to feel tired . . .

A woman's scream sounded from upstairs, yanking June from her thoughts. One of her girls was in trouble. She bounded from the chair and ran up the stairway. As she reached the top of the stairs a shout for help came from the first door to her left.

In almost one movement, June ran to the door and flung it open. Inside, a cowboy she barely recognized was on his feet, fully dressed, and pointing a gun at a girl who called herself 'Tammy.' Tammy was lying in bed, covering herself with a thin blanket.

'What's going on here?' June tried to keep the fear from her voice.

The cowboy used his gun as a pointer. 'This girlie ain't doin' what I tol' her.'

'I'm sorry, Miss June, but he was gettin' rough, I mean, real rough.' Tammy was a short, thin girl with stringy dark hair and skin the color of water.

June began her usual talk for these situations, 'Look, cowboy, I know you're here for a good time. Nothing wrong with that, but — '

The cowboy turned and pointed the gun at her. The weapon shook in his hand. 'Git! Ya hear! This ain't no concern of yours!'

June held up her palms. 'Please — '

'I said git! Ya don't leave now, I'll shoot ya and then I kill the girlie!'

June closed the door and ran down the stairway. She paused briefly on the last stair to catch her breath and then hurried to the bar where Fred, the bartender, was talking with three customers.

The woman spoke in an anxious voice that was almost a sob. 'Fred, there's a man upstairs with a gun pointed at Tammy. He's threatening to kill her.'

Fred, an overweight, balding man of about fifty, looked scared. For a moment his tongue made an awkward journey across his top lip. A look of forced amusement suddenly waved across his face. 'Sounds like a dove is about to get a feather plucked; that's no concern of mine.'

The three men at the bar guffawed and gave the woman lewd glances. June stepped away from them and shouted to the entire saloon. 'There's a girl upstairs in trouble, some jasper is holding a gun on her, are any of you so-called men gonna do anything about it?'

This time, not a single face turned toward the woman. June shouted a string of obscenities at the men who were mostly staring at cards or at the walls of the Lady Luck. A voice suddenly responded to her insults. 'The sheriff's right next door.'

June ran from the saloon. Holding her skirts over her ankles, she ran to the stage depot, which was next door to the saloon. Sheriff Amos Santell was standing there with another man, who was wearing a deputy's badge. She didn't know who the man was but he looked like he could back up that piece of tin on his shirt.

The sheriff realized immediately that something was wrong. He didn't bother with a greeting. 'What's the trouble, June?'

'Some jasper is holding a gun on one of my girls.'

'Where?' Santell asked.

'Top of the stairway, first door on the left.'

The two men ran toward the Lady Luck. June closed her eyes for a moment. When she opened them again she saw Phoebe Gibson, a woman who worked at the stage depot, staring at her with strong disapproval.

'You belong back in the saloon,' Phoebe declared.

The anger had left June Day to be replaced by fatigue and resignation. She looked around for a moment and gave a laugh that was devoid of any humor or happiness.

'You're right.' June returned to the Lady Luck and the life that awaited her there.

★ ★ ★

Amos Santell and his new deputy stormed through the batwings of the Lady Luck and ran up the stairs. They stopped at the door June had indicated and, instinctively, drew their guns. 'We can't take him by surprise,' the sheriff whispered, 'we might scare the fool and he'll pull the trigger. Gotta think first 'bout the girl.'

Santell knocked lightly on the door and received a loud, angry response. 'Go away!'

'It's the law,' Santell replied. 'We're coming in to have a little talk.'

For a moment, the voice inside the

room went quiet. Dehner thought he heard the sound of bed springs but couldn't be sure. When the voice sounded again, it was more subdued but no less threatening. 'Ya don't need no guns for jawin'. Leave your guns in the hall. Walk in slow, like, or a little dove named Tammy will get a big bullet in her pretty head.'

Santell and Dehner looked at each other, shrugged their shoulders and placed their guns on the floor. Santell spoke in a calm voice. 'We're coming in like ya said.'

The two lawmen entered the room. They saw a medium-sized, unshaven man with a touch of gray running through his stubble, standing beside a bed with a pistol pointed at a young woman, who was cowering on her knees in the middle of the mattress covering herself with a blanket.

'What's your name, cowboy?' the sheriff asked.

'Folks call me Wyoming.'

Neither lawman believed that claim. The gunman was probably a crook with circulars out on him. He had probably never been anywhere close to Wyoming.

Dehner smiled in a friendly manner and hooked his thumbs on his belt, making himself look non-threatening. He strolled around to the opposite side of the bed where he could face Wyoming from across the mattress. The girl was between him and the gunman. Santell was still standing near the opened door.

'There just aren't enough women in the West, Wyoming.' Dehner continued to smile as he spoke. 'Not much sense in hurting the gals that we do have, why, that might discourage other pretty girls from coming here.'

Dehner moved closer to the bed. The gunman took two steps closer on his side, pointing his gun directly at him. 'Maybe we're better off without some cheap floozies.'

Dehner gave Wyoming a hard stare. His voice turned serious. 'So, you think Tammy is a cheap floozie? Is that why you hit her on the side of her face? Only a coward would hit a woman.'

'I never — '

Dehner bent over and nodded toward Tammy. 'Then where did that bruise come from?'

Keeping his gun on the detective, Wyoming bent over to see the bruise. Dehner lifted the bed and slammed it against the gunman. Tammy screamed as she rolled off the mattress and on to the floor. Wyoming stumbled backwards giving a loud curse, which was followed by a cry of pain as Santell landed a punch to the side of his head. Wyoming hit the floor only a few feet from Tammy. The sheriff grabbed the gunman's weapon and ordered him to get up.

Dehner helped Tammy to her feet. To his surprise, the saloon girl was wearing a dress. The straps were pulled down, leaving her shoulders bare. Why had Tammy been holding a blanket over herself?

Sheriff Santell had a different question for the girl. 'Ma'am, did ya want to press charges against this owlhoot?'

Tammy pulled her dress straps back in place. 'No, Sheriff. That won't be necessary.'

That answer surprised Amos. 'Excuse me, ma'am, but that's what ya need to do. Why, if his gun had gone off — '

'It ain't loaded!' Wyoming was now standing up, though he was a bit wobbly.

'What?' The sheriff took a closer look at Wyoming's six-shooter. 'He's right.'

'I was jus' havin' a little fun with the girlie. Can I have my gun back?'

Amos looked out the door; June was standing in the hallway, holding the guns that belonged to him and Dehner. 'Sure, ya can have your gun back, mister. Soon as ya show me your horse.'

'Whaddya wanna see my nag for?'

''Cause you're getting on that nag and riding outta town right now.' Amos pointed at the doorway with his thumb. 'Come on!'

After the three men left the room, Amos retrieved the guns from June and thanked her as he and his deputy holstered the weapons. 'June, think you can take care of that Tammy girl OK?'

'I think so, Sheriff. Thanks for helping . . . you and your deputy.'

That statement opened the door for Santell to introduce Dehner to the woman but the sheriff didn't notice. Other concerns dominated his thoughts. 'That Tammy was acting right strange. Think she might be a bit touched in the head?'

'I don't think so, Sheriff Santell,' June replied. 'Having a gun pointed at you and some moron shouting that he might kill you could make anyone act strange.'

Santell smiled and shrugged his shoulders. 'Guess ya got a point.' The smile vanished as he turned to Wyoming. 'Come on, move!'

Dehner touched his hat and nodded at June as she entered the room to attend to Tammy. He then began to follow the sheriff and Wyoming. He stayed behind them as they walked down the stairway. Wyoming complained about his treatment. The sheriff said nothing.

Wyoming's complaints continued as

they walked through the saloon. 'I ain't done nothin' wrong, 'cept have fun. It must be agin the law for a man to have fun in this here town!'

Santell suddenly broke his silence of the last couple of minutes. 'Yeah, Wyoming, I guess ya need to find yourself a town that's more so-phistecated!'

The sheriff tripped Wyoming. The thug hit the floor and scrambled to get up but Santell kicked him in the area of the anatomy nature provided for such assaults. This time Wyoming hit the floor face first. The saloon erupted into laughter. Santell picked the thug up by the scruff of his neck, walked him to the batwings, and threw him out of the saloon. The laughter got even louder.

Dehner followed the sheriff outside as he stood over Wyoming and ordered him on to his feet. Wyoming complied, this time without complaining.

'Where's your horse?' the sheriff asked.

Wyoming pointed at a black that was tethered to the hitch rail in front of the saloon. 'Right there.'

'Ride.' Santell's voice was low and firm. 'I'd better never see you in this town again. Never!'

Wyoming mounted his black as harsh laughter still resounded from inside the Lady Luck. He didn't look back as he spurred his horse and began to gallop out of town.

As they watched the thug ride off Dehner asked the sheriff,

'Do you know if Wyoming, or whatever his real name is, was in town long?'

'Rode in yesterday. Probably jus' passing through. I suspect he was on his way to do a job . . . not an honest job mind you. I know the type.'

The sheriff of Hardin gave his companion a lopsided grin. 'Ya know, Dehner, human bein's are strange animals. In a few days Wyoming will have forgotten all 'bout holding a gun on Tammy. But getting his behind kicked in a saloon and having a whole bunch of fellers laugh at him, he'll never forgit that. Wyoming won't be back in our town anytime soon.'

For a moment, Dehner and Santell reflected on the odd duties demanded of a lawman. Then they heard the gunshots.

13

'The sheriff's right next door.' John Latchman spoke tonelessly as he sat at a table alone in the Lady Luck. No one looked his way. Nobody cared where the voice came from.

Latchman watched June Day scamper from the saloon. A few moments later, Amos Santell and Rance Dehner ran through the batwings and up the stairway.

John got up, leaving his paid-for drink on the table. He left the saloon quickly but not too quickly. He couldn't call attention to himself.

Outside, Latchman's eyes briefly rolled sideways. June Day had her back to him. She appeared to be talking with a lady at the stage depot. Good. He didn't know if June remembered him from his occasional patronage of the Lady Luck or not. But it would be best if no one recalled seeing him in the saloon on this particular afternoon.

Latchman crossed the street, walking at a brisker pace. So far everything was going as planned. From the information he and Rose had obtained from Max Chumley that morning, he knew that Dehner would be doing the afternoon round with Santell. And that round usually consisted of meeting the 4.30 p.m. stage. When possible, the sheriff or his deputy always met the stage. They wanted to look over any newcomers.

John suddenly realized that he was almost running down the boardwalk to the sheriff's office. He slowed his pace. There was no big hurry. After all, he had paid a drifter and a dove good money to create a diversion and keep the two lawmen occupied.

The lawyer stopped outside the sheriff's office and inhaled deeply. He tried to look relaxed; he was the town's barrister, performing an unpleasant but necessary duty.

He strolled into the office with a

casual gait. His efforts were wasted on Max Chumley. The deputy was delivering an animated monologue to Rod Baker, the editor, reporter, and salesman for the *Hardin Bugle*.

'You know, sometimes a lawman has gotta be sort of an actor. That's what I had to do in order to capture . . . ' Max suddenly noticed the newcomer. 'Howdy Mr Latchman, are you here to see your client?'

'Yes. Sorry to interrupt your interview.'

'That's no problem. Say, have you met Mr Rod Baker, the editor of — '

'I know Mr Baker.' John's tone was buoyant. 'How's the newspaper business, sir?'

Baker was a short man with an unusually large head and a voice that sounded like a Shakespearean actor. He always seemed to have a pad and pencil in hand or, at least, nearby. 'I will be quite happy when the railroad finally arrives in our fair town.'

The lawyer smiled and nodded. He knew that Baker was having a tough time selling advertising to the small town merchants, who found word of mouth to be a very effective and economical way of hawking their goods and services.

Max lifted a set of keys off a nail that protruded from the side of the office desk. 'I'll be right back, Mr Baker.'

Max escorted the lawyer through a door and into the jail area. There were three cells. Two were empty. One contained Ash Carrick.

Chumley opened the occupied cell. 'I'll be right outside, Mr Latchman. Jus' call out when you're done.'

'Thanks, Deputy.' John watched as Chumley locked the cell door and returned to the office area.

The lawyer turned to Ash Carrick and was shocked. The man's nose was broken and one eye was almost swollen shut. For the first time, Latchman began to doubt that people would buy the story he had carefully plotted out. But he had to make it work; so much was at stake.

Carrick got up from his cot. 'Thanks for seeing me, Counselor.'

'Good to meet you, Mr Carrick.'

The two men did a quick hand shake, then Carrick added, 'You know, I was once a lawyer myself.'

'Oh.' Latchman noticed that Carrick looked a bit unsteady on his feet. He hoped the man didn't sit down again. This scheme would be easier to pull off with Ash Carrick standing up.

'I need you to do a favor for me, Counselor.' Carrick's entire body seemed to acquire new energy. He was excited by whatever he was about to say.

'And what favor is that, Mr Carrick?'

'Well, it has nothing to do with your profession. Nothing personal, but I have no interest in receiving legal services from you.'

'I'm glad to hear that, Mr Carrick.' John reached into his pocket, carefully removed a small knife and dropped it on to the floor. He then unbuttoned his coat and yanked a pistol from out of a shoulder holster. 'You see, I have no interest in performing legal services for you. Nothing personal.'

Latchman pumped three bullets into Ash Carrick's chest. Carrick stumbled backwards, and then took a few steps toward John Latchman as if attempting to attack his killer. The shock began to drain from his face as his body collapsed.

John Latchman allowed himself a quick smile. 'You landed face down, friend,' he whispered. 'Good thing your nose was already broken.'

Max Chumley came scrambling into the jail area, the newspaperman right behind him. 'What happened?' Chumley fumbled with the jail keys, finally locating the right one.

Latchman glared accusingly at the deputy as he entered the cell followed by Rod Baker. 'The prisoner attacked me with a knife. Who examined this man for weapons before he was jailed?'

'I did!'

Though he maintained an angry expression, the lawyer was jubilant. An old lawdog like Amos Santell would be hard to confound, not so a green kid. 'And you found no weapons?'

'No!' Max sounded bewildered and humiliated. Only seconds ago, he had been the town's hero, now . . .

The lawyer bore in on his target. 'Are you sure? Absolutely certain? Could you place your right hand on a Bible and swear that it was impossible for Ash Carrick to have a knife concealed on his body when he entered this jail cell?'

'Well, maybe not, I don't know.'

Santell and Dehner came running into the jail area and entered the cell, creating a suffocating space. 'What's going on?' the sheriff shouted at no one person in particular.

John Latchman had established his dominance in this situation and wasn't about to surrender it. 'Sheriff, your prisoner had a knife concealed on his person. He tried to kill me with it.'

Amos Santell looked around. 'Where's this here knife?'

With a dramatic flourish, John

Latchman crouched over the body of Ash Carrick, grabbed it by the shoulder and turned it part way over, revealing a blood-drenched knife on the floor. A look of intensity filled the lawyer's eyes as he addressed Amos Santell. 'Your deputy just confessed to me that he can't swear he checked the prisoner close enough to find a small knife like this one.' He returned the body to the floor as if concluding a lecture.

The lawyer stood up, his voice still heavy with righteous indignation. 'If you need to ask me any questions regarding this tragedy, I will make myself available. Good day, gentlemen.'

As he exited from the cell, Latchman saw Rod Baker writing furiously on his pad. A feeling of smugness enveloped the lawyer. Max Chumley's name would still be on the front page of the paper. But the article would be much different than what the deputy had once thought.

14

Earl Whitney strolled into the living room of his ranch house, carrying a cup of coffee on a saucer, the conclusion of his supper. From the dining room, he could hear Esther, the cook, and Leona clearing the dishes.

The rancher gazed across the living room to the grand piano, which dominated almost one half of the large room. In an hour or so, his wife would be giving Leona lessons on the piano. The girl was a fast learner and both she and Rose had beautiful voices. They would be playing and singing some of the old hymns. He looked forward to that.

He placed the coffee cup down on the side table of his favorite chair. On that same table lay an edition of *A Tale of Two Cities*.

'Charles Dickens,' Earl said to

himself. 'What a way with words that man has!'

Hoof beats sounded from outside. Someone was approaching the ranch house. Earl whispered a few curse words. His day had been a hard one and he sensed that the couple hours of enjoyment that were now in front of him were about to be marred.

He walked to the large window that looked out on the ranch and pulled back a curtain. What he saw confirmed his worst suspicion.

'Do we have a visitor, Earl?'

The rancher turned to his wife, who had just entered the room. 'Yes, I'm afraid so, it's John Latchman.'

'Hardin is fortunate to have a lawyer. Many small western towns do not.'

Earl didn't work too hard at keeping the irritation out of his voice. 'Yes, yes, of course.'

But the rancher did manage to sound moderately cheerful as he answered the knock on the door. 'A pleasure to see you, Mr Latchman, please come in.'

John Latchman removed his hat as he stepped inside. 'Good evening, Mr Whitney.' He smiled at Rose Whitney and nodded his head in an elaborate manner that was almost a bow. 'Mrs Whitney.'

'It is a pleasure to see you, Mr Latchman,' Rose smiled politely. 'I'm afraid we have finished supper. But would you care for some coffee?'

'No thank you,' John replied hastily. 'I purposely held off on this visit because I didn't wish to interrupt your evening meal. But something important happened in town, today. Something you both should know about.'

Earl walked away from the closed door and to the center of the living room where John Latchman was now standing close to Rose. 'And what might that be, Mr Latchman?'

'As the two of you may know, Ash Carrick asked to see me. Of course, I wanted nothing to do with such a monster. But I am Hardin's only lawyer and — '

'Yes, yes,' Earl cut in impatiently.

'Well, while I was interviewing Carrick in his cell, the man attacked me with a knife! Fortunately, I was wearing my shoulder holster. I tried to shoot only to wound but at that close a range — '

'You killed him,' there was a note of anxiety in Rose's voice.

'Yes, I'm afraid so.'

'It may be for the best, Mr Latchman.' Rose was able to keep a look of relief from her face. 'If Ash Carrick had lived, there would have been a trial and Leona would have had to testify. That would have been hard on the girl.'

Earl Whitney appeared confused by the news. 'Tell me, Mr Latchman, why would this Carrick fellow try to kill you? It doesn't make sense. After all, he asked to see you. He must have wanted you to defend him.'

Latchman nodded his head, this time in a solemn manner. 'An hour or so after the shooting, Sheriff Santell came to my office and asked me that exact question.'

'Was Rance Dehner with him?' Rose asked anxiously.

'Yes.'

'So, what did you tell them?' The irritation was returning to Earl's voice.

'Before attacking me, Carrick mentioned that he had once been a lawyer himself. He must have been forced out of the profession for some act of gross misconduct. Carrick knew he was going to hang anyway. So, his depraved mind decided upon an act of revenge against lawyers.'

'That certainly makes sense,' Rose replied immediately.

Earl Whitney slowly caressed his mustache. 'I suppose so.'

'Did Sheriff Santell and Mr Dehner agree with your theory?'

Latchman caught the tension in Rose Whitney's voice. 'They didn't express an opinion, which of course is appropriate to their duty as lawmen. But I do believe that they, at the very least, accept my reasoning.'

Rose smiled politely but she wasn't happy with the roundabout answer to her question. The woman quietly assured herself that the action she would soon take was necessary.

'I know the two of you will want to make Leona aware of this development.' Latchman took a step toward the door. 'I will be leaving now. I wish you both a pleasant evening.'

Earl made a quick journey to the door and opened it. 'Thank you for coming by with the news, Mr Latchman.'

He closed the door with a slightly disgusted look on his face. 'Be careful around that man, my dear.'

'What do you mean?'

'The gleam in his eyes when he looks at you could light up a dark cave.'

Rose laughed, and shook her head. 'Earl, you are being foolish.'

John Latchman was really the foolish one, she thought while continuing to ease her husband's suspicions. Latchman fancied himself a clever deceiver but wasn't. She needed Latchman but could not allow him to call the shots. For that reason, she had not even told the lawyer about the plans that would be initiated tomorrow. Plans to murder Rance Dehner.

15

Rose Whitney was sitting at her desk in the room used for an office when she heard a knock on the front door of the ranch house. The timing couldn't have been better. Leona was outside the office in the hallway doing some light dusting as she often did in the early afternoon while Samuel was sleeping.

Rose shouted good-naturedly through the open doorway. 'Leona, would you mind seeing who is at the door?'

'Not at all, Mrs Whitney,' Leona shouted back.

A few moments later, Leona returned, looking and sounding a bit confused. 'Mrs Whitney, there are two gents here askin' for food. Should I — '

'I'll handle this. You can get back to your dusting. Thank you.' Rose smiled at Leona as she left the office. This plan was getting off to a good start. Rose

Whitney wanted at least one other person to see the two strangers and understand why they had been allowed inside. Leona was the perfect witness. Earl and all of the hands had now finished lunch and were back at work.

As she approached the door, Rose braced herself. She had hired these men through an intermediary. She hadn't met them herself.

Even braced, Rose was not quite prepared for the two scraggly saddle-bums who were standing on the front porch of the ranch as she opened the door. Both men had dark hair that covered half of their ears and almost touched their shoulders. They were unshaven and both looked at her with silly grins. She had been told that they were brothers but was unprepared for two men who looked so much alike.

'Afternoon, ma'am, would you be Mrs Rose Whitney?'

'Yes, I am.'

'My name's Sid Slocum; this here is my brother, Sam. We've been hearin' all

153

over 'bout what an uplifting touch of heaven the Whitney ranch can be for poor wayfarers such as us.'

Sam Slocum looked upwards in a dramatic gesture. 'We've been told this here ranch is jus' stuffed with the spirit of Christian charity.'

'Well, I hope that's true,' Rose replied.

'So do we,' Sid shot back. 'You see, my brother and I are ridin' the grub line.'

'You mean you are looking for work in order to eat?' Rose asked.

'Not exactly,' Sid replied slowly. 'We're not much inclined toward the workin' part of it.'

'Yeah,' Sam picked up on his brother's point. 'But if you feed us, we'll get outta your hair right quick.'

Sid's smile brightened. 'That'll save you the bother of havin' to fire us later on.'

'Well, at the Whitney ranch we never turn away anyone who is hungry.' Rose spoke in a voice louder than necessary. She wanted Leona to hear her. Rose now had some backup if her husband came into the ranch house and wanted to know who these two owlhoots were.

'Thank you, ma'am,' Sam picked up on the woman's cue and also lifted his voice. 'You are storin' up treasures in heaven.'

'But we can't give you nothin',' Sid quickly added.

Rose stepped back and allowed the two men into the house. The signal that the intermediary had given her was that the two men would say they were riding the grub line but didn't want to work. Rose had originally thought the notion a bit too odd. But looking at Sam and Sid Slocum, the woman realized the signal was totally believable.

Rose looked back down the hallway at Leona and shrugged her shoulders in a comical manner while making a silly face. She then turned to the Slocum brothers. 'Follow me, please. I'll take you to the kitchen. Our cook is taking her break before getting started on the evening meal.'

★ ★ ★

Leona smiled back at Rose, who escorted the two men down the eastern wing of the house, opposite from where Leona was dusting. Mrs Whitney really is a good person, Leona thought. Sure, Will Maltin was right. She was not as easy to get along with as her husband, but then Will often called Earl Whitney his second father. 'He can't get 'long much with his first father,' the young woman whispered to herself as she moved into the living room to continue her work.

Thoughts of Will Maltin flooded her mind. Will sure had a strange relationship with his father. Was that why he was so uncertain about his aunt? After all, Rose Whitney was Bradford Maltin's sister. The young woman wondered why Will couldn't be content just to have a father, any father. Leona had never known hers and had only had a mother for the first seven years of her life.

Samuel's cries intruded on her

thoughts. The young woman left her dusting and headed for the baby, knowing Mrs Whitney wouldn't object to the delay. She really is a nice person, Leona thought to herself once again.

* * *

Rose walked the newcomers hastily through the dining room and into the kitchen where she pointed to a large wooden table. The two men dutifully sat down as Rose ladled out two bowls of stew from a black kettle on the stove and placed them in front of the two strange guests and then sat down with them.

Serving food to roustabouts was nothing new at the Whitney ranch. Earl Whitney's sense of charity was known throughout the area. Still, Rose rarely spent much time conversing with saddle-bums. Her presence here would strike most people as unusual. She needed to make this quick.

'Sam and Sid Slocum, are those your real names?'

Both men appeared more interested in the stew than in the question. After swallowing a large portion, Sam answered. 'No, ma'am. You see, a man's gotta be sente-mental 'bout somethun.'

Sid nodded his head in agreement. 'Only bein' sentimental is kinda tough when you kill men for a livin'.'

Sam continued, 'So we get sente-mental 'bout our names. We take new names for each job and the names are always an alliter-ation. Alliter-ation means — '

'I know what it means!' Rose cut in.

Sid talked while chewing his food. 'For our last job we was Brian and Bob Buckley. Sounds right distinguished, don't you think? It fit too. The last guy we killed was a right distinguished fella. A pillar of the church.'

'Yeah,' Sam chimed in. 'Now the poor fella is buried behind the church.'

'Are you men always successful with your, ah, assignments?'

This time, Sid finished chewing on his food and swallowed before answering. 'Yep. We owe our success to our carefully crafted method of doin' a job.'

Sam suddenly remembered that his hat was still on. He took it off and placed it on the table, then nudged his brother to do the same. 'We ain't your average killers, Mrs Whitney!'

'What do you mean?'

'Most killers are gunfighters,' Sam explained. 'They pride themselves on their speed with a gun. For them, a good time is to step out in the middle of the street and look their prey right in the eye and have it out, man to man, to see who is the fastest draw. Me and Sid don't much care for that approach.'

Sid raised an index finger as if making an important point. 'That's a right dangerous way to go 'bout the job. Not professional at all, and hardly what a discernin' client would be lookin' for. The results are jus' too uncertain.'

Sam shook his head. 'Well, in our case, not too uncertain. Neither one of us is exactly lightnin' on the draw. So, we set our man up. One of us gets the gent in a spot where the other can ambush him. Not noble, but effective.'

'The man I want you to kill is named Rance Dehner. He is a deputy sheriff in Hardin.'

'Whoopee,' Sid exclaimed. 'Deputy sheriffs is our favorite targets.'

'Why is that?'

'Deputy sheriffs all have them routines.' Sam scooped up the last of the stew with his spoon. 'Makes them easy to set up.'

'And folks don't get all weepy over dead deputies,' Sid added. 'Now, sheriffs is different. Lotsa folks get upset when you put a bullet or two into a sheriff. They jaw on 'bout what a fine servant of the people he was, all that stuff. Sometimes, they get so riled they get up a posse and come after you.'

Sam's face beamed with happiness. 'But nobody carries on when a deputy gets plugged. I'll bet a lot of folks don't even know this deputy's name. We should have him cold for you right soon. Say, do you suppose we could have us a second bowl of that stew?'

16

Sam and Sid Slocum sat at a table in the Lady Luck saloon. Sam chortled as he poured himself another drink. 'This here job is almost too easy. We've only been in town a day and a half and already we got Deputy Rance Dehner's routines down.'

His brother smiled contentedly. 'It's a sad thing when a man's life is chained to a clock. No time to stop and smell the flowers.'

'Yep,' Sam agreed. 'A deputy is not much better off than a farmer. Up with the sun, feedin' chickens, milkin' cows, and plantin' stuff.'

'Routines destroy a man's soul.' Sid's voice took on a philosophical tone. 'Sometimes I think we do a man a favor by destroyin' his body.'

The batwings were pushed open and two men entered the saloon. One was a huge man, wearing a blacksmith's apron; the other was a lanky kid.

'Hey Larry, this here is a special day!' the blacksmith yelled at the bartender on duty that night.

'What's the occasion, Horace?'

Horace Riley walked up to the bar, his arm around the shoulder of his young friend. 'Why, this is the birthday of my helper, Del Burgess. Seventeen years old, today!'

'Well!' Larry shook Del's hand. 'This calls for a drink on the house.'

The blacksmith tossed a few coins on to the bar. 'Knew you'd say that. I'm buying the second drink.' Horace lowered his voice to a mild bellow. 'Del, use what's left to buy yourself a good time with one of the pretty little girls they got here.' He gave the kid a lewd wink.

'Gotta git back to the livery.' Horace looked around the bar. 'Don't none of you gents worry. I ain't leaving your nags alone for long.' The blacksmith waved to the patrons, most of whom he knew, as he left the Lady Luck.

Del Burgess sipped nervously at his beer for a few minutes and then addressed the bartender in a low voice. 'Larry, I appreciate the free drink and all, but one beer is enough for me.'

'Sure.'

'And that other stuff Horace talked about. Horace means well. He's taught me a lot and he's my boss and all but . . . '

The bartender smiled kindly. 'Everyone knows what a show-off Horace is. Likes to talk about how much money he's got. Good thing nobody from the bank is here right now. They'd have laughed in his face.'

Larry slid the coins back to Del. 'It's your birthday, kid. You spend the money any way you want.'

Del's eyes brightened as he pocketed the money. 'Thanks. Think I'll buy somethun nice for Leona. You know, her birthday ain't far off — '

'That boy ain't got much good taste, huh, Butch?'

'No, Cotton, he sure don't.'

The voices came from two barflies standing at the bar a few feet away from Del. They were both liquored up and looking for trouble.

'Shoot, Butch, that pup turned down all of the gals here for that Leona tramp. At least a dove is honest about her line of work.'

Cotton raised his voice. 'Of course, just maybe he became a daddy 'fore his seventeenth birthday. Once a man gets usta getting his fun for free, it don't seem right paying for it.'

Del took a few angry steps toward the barflies. 'You jaspers talk too much.'

Butch laughed mockingly. 'You talk pretty tough for a green kid who ain't carrying a gun.'

'I don't need no gun to handle you jaspers.'

The Slocum brothers had been carefully watching how this scene played out. Sid whispered, 'Dear brother, I do think our good luck is continuin' at a strong pace.'

'Let's git to it!'

The Slocums walked toward the bar. Sid shouted out, 'If you fellas is lookin' for someone who is carryin' a gun, we'd be happy to oblige.'

Cotton eyed the newcomers angrily. 'Who're you guys?'

'Saddlebums, jus' like you two,' Sam shot back. 'But we're saddlebums who believe that a man should be able to celebrate his birthday without bein' bothered.'

'Yep.' Sid nodded his head approvingly. 'Guess we're a higher class of saddlebum than you two.'

Cotton's anger ratcheted up. 'We'll just see 'bout — '

The bartender began to reach for a peacemaker he kept under the bar. Butch spotted the move, grabbed a beer mug he had just emptied, and smashed it on Larry's head. As the bartender screamed in pain and dropped to the floor, Sam delivered a punch to Butch's eye. Butch staggered backwards, folded his hands into fists and moved toward his attacker.

Del and Cotton began to exchange blows. It occurred to Del that this was his first barroom brawl. Horace Riley had often recounted his many such brawls and made each one sound like a great time.

Del didn't find it all that much fun.

* * *

Rance Dehner left the sheriff's office with Max Chumley. The two deputies were doing the early evening round together.

'Pleasant night,' Dehner said.

'Yep,' came the indifferent reply.

Max Chumley had been quiet and withdrawn since Ash Carrick was killed while in a jail cell. The relationship between Max and his boss had become uneasy.

Dehner felt more than a little bit guilty about the situation. He once again questioned his decision to use Chumley in his ploy to trap Ash Carrick. Yes, Max had the imagination needed to carry out the scheme. But Dehner hadn't considered how dazzled the young man would be by his status as town hero.

'He's right, you know.' Max's voice was little more than a whisper.

'Who's right?'

'Sheriff Santell.' Chumley pressed his lips together for a moment and then continued. 'He was right. I was jus' plain loco not to have searched Ash Carrick for a weapon like a small knife. I made a fool of myself and made the sheriff look bad. He's got ever' right to be mad at me.'

'Being a lawman is hard, Max.' Dehner spoke as the two men walked toward the Lady Luck. An average round consisted of at least two stops at the saloon, the town's main source of trouble. 'You're going to look foolish now and again, might as well get used to it.'

'I'm not sure I'm cut out to be a lawman, maybe I should — '

A cry of pain and the sound of a fight blasted out from the Lady Luck. The two deputies began to run toward the saloon. As they darted inside, they were greeted by loud sounds from the patrons who were cheering and laughing as a fight was going on near the bar.

'Seems to be five men involved,' Dehner said to his companion. 'I recognize Del Burgess, you know any of the others?'

'Two of 'em look a bit familiar. Don't know their names, though.'

The lawmen hurried toward the scuffle. Dehner took out his Colt and fired toward the ceiling, being careful not to hit the wagonwheel chandelier. He wondered, casually, how many bullets had been fired into the ceiling over the years.

'Break it up, right now!' he shouted.

The two barflies were outnumbered, beaten, and more than happy to comply with Dehner's order. The bartender was back on his feet and angry. His account of how the brawl started accurately put all of the blame on Cotton and Butch.

'He's lyin'.' Cotton looked at the bartender accusingly and then shifted his gaze to the deputy. Like his partner, Cotton was on his feet but none too steady. 'We was jus' expressin' an opinion. A man's got a right to say what's on his mind.'

'That's right.' Max Chumley's voice was low and firm. 'You two gents are leaving to express your opinions in another town.'

'Wha — ?' Cotton said.

'Leave town. Both of you, now.'

Butch stood up as straight as he could, striking a self-righteous pose, or trying to. 'We's in town looking for honest work.'

Max laughed contemptuously. 'I've been watching you jaspers. You've been in town for two weeks, maybe more. The only work you've looked for is lifting your elbows. Leave now, this is the last time I'm gonna tell you.'

Cotton and Butch part walked and part stumbled out of the saloon. Max and Dehner both watched over the batwings as the two troublemakers mounted their horses, which were tied up outside of the saloon, and rode out of town.

Del Burgess looked embarrassed as he lightly caressed his sore jaw. 'Thanks guys,' he said to the Slocum brothers. The young man turned to the two deputies and explained, 'These gents helped me out when I got in more trouble than I could handle.'

Larry pointed at Sam from behind the bar. 'I was lying on the floor but could see this gent deliver a roundhouse to the fool who clobbered me with a beer mug.'

Sam smiled at the bartender. 'Common decency demanded that I take action. Why, usin' a wonderful invention like a beer mug as a weapon! What's this world comin' to?'

Sid nodded his head in vigorous agreement. 'The practice had to be nipped in the bud, otherwise it could have led to the collapse of western civilization.'

The bartender, the two deputies, and Del Burgess all laughed for few moments, then Max Chumley asked the two strangers for their names.

The brothers answered in unison. 'Sam and Sid Slocum, at your service.'

There was more laughter, which Dehner spoke over. 'What brings you gents to Hardin?'

Sid replied, 'We is jus' two worthless saddlebums who is lookin' for a town where we can settle down, turn over a new leaf, and become two worthless barflies.'

Sam hastily added, 'But don't worry, Hardin is not the town for us. We'll be ridin' out soon.'

'We could never be happy here,' Sid stated emphatically. 'Hardin may be a small place, but it's already got a church and a school. Folks who go to church are too upright for us and folks who go to school are too smart to come near a pair of no-goods like me and my brother.'

Del Burgess shook the hands of both newcomers. 'I'm sure happy you no-goods were in town tonight. Afraid I'm no good when it comes to a barroom brawl.'

'Don't worry,' Sam replied. 'You'll

171

improve with experience.'

Sid cocked his head in a thoughtful manner. 'On the other hand, maybe you're better off without the experience. You could end up like me and my brother.'

The conversation continued in that vein for several more minutes and then the two deputies left the saloon along with Del Burgess. The encounter with the Slocum brothers had left the three men in a good mood. As the lawmen said goodbye to Del and continued their round, Dehner felt thankful to the Slocums. They had brought some laughter into Max Chumley's life at a time when he very much needed it.

* * *

An hour later, Sam and Sid were back at the same table slowly nursing their drinks. 'Worked like a charm, brother, Dehner thinks we're harmless saddle-bums with a touch of the Good Samaritan.'

Sid smiled at the amber liquid in front of him. 'Yep. I say we move tonight, when Dehner does the 1 a.m. round. That's when we kill him.'

17

Sid Slocum climbed on to the roof of the Lady Luck and pulled the ladder he had stolen up after him. He bent down into a jack knife position and made his way to the front of the building.

He lay down flat and examined the scene below. The boardwalks were empty. His last glance inside the Lady Luck had been a few minutes ago. The saloon had only a scattering of customers left. This plan was going just fine.

Sid experienced the rush of excitement that always coursed through him just before he killed a man. He was a much better shot than his brother, so Sam got the job of setting the target up; Sid got to pull the trigger.

Sid caressed the Henry that snuggled against his right shoulder and tried to calm his mind by going over the particular circumstances of this killing.

Sam would be hanging around outside the saloon. Dehner would soon be coming by doing the 1 a.m. round. Sam would get him to cross the street, where they would be out of eye range of the saloon's batwings but still close enough to the light from the saloon to make for a good shot. As he had done so often in the past, Sid would wave to his brother before he fired. Sam would hit the ground and Dehner would get hit by a shot from the Henry. Sam would then draw his Remington .44 and finish Dehner off.

Of course there were a slew of unknowns and that is what increased the excitement and interest for Sid Slocum. Max Chumley might be making the round with Dehner as he had before. The Slocums had picked up some loose talk in the saloon earlier that evening. Seems that Chumley had bungled a job good and the sheriff now wanted Dehner to be with him whenever he did a round.

Sid laughed softly. If he was with

Dehner on the next round, Chumley wouldn't be making any more blunders. When Dehner went down, Max Chumley would naturally look upwards trying to see where the shot had come from. He would be an easy target for Sam's Remington.

There were fresh horses tied up behind the saloon. After making sure the job was finished, Sam would hightail it behind the Lady Luck and the two men would make a fast exit.

Sid nervously caressed the Henry and tried to think of anything else that might get in the way of this job. Most of the men still inside the Lady Luck were either upstairs with a girlie or too drunk to cause him and his brother any problems. There was Larry, who kept a peacemaker under the bar, but the barkeep had taken a hard blow on the noggin just a few hours ago. He was probably moving pretty slow.

Sid spotted his brother coming out of the saloon and his nervousness vanished, to be replaced by an intense concentration. The Henry became an extension of his body. He was ready for the kill.

★　★　★

Rance Dehner was happy to see Sam Slocum leaning against the front of the Lady Luck. A few laughs were always appreciated in the late hours.

But as Sam began to walk briskly toward Dehner and Max Chumley, Dehner's cheer was replaced by curiosity. 'Slocum seems to want to talk to us about something.'

'Yep.' Max quickly looked around. 'I wonder where his brother is.'

'Evenin', Deputies.' Sam's words almost collided with each other. The two lawmen nodded.

'I noticed somethin' that might interest you gents,' Sam continued to speak in haste.

'What might that be?'

'Two jaspers jus' rode into town. They're in the saloon. Look like real hardcases. I was goin' back to the hotel when I spotted the saddle-bags on their horses.'

'What about the saddle-bags?' Dehner asked.

'Them things are bulgin',' Sam answered. 'I think there's money inside. Looks to me like them fellers jus' robbed themselves a bank somewheres earlier today and now feel they're far enough away to stop for a spell.'

Dehner's face crunched up. 'Doesn't seem likely that two bank robbers would leave the money stashed in their saddle-bags while they went inside a saloon.'

Sam cocked his head to one side. 'Maybe at one time, but them dime novels have changed that. Now, ever' fool on earth thinks he can be a great criminal. The standards ain't what they usta be.'

Dehner pointed toward the saloon. 'Let's step inside and get a look at those two hardcases.'

Sam Slocum held up an arm as if blocking the lawmen's path into the

Lady Luck. 'Why don't we check them saddle-bags first? Iffin' I'm wrong there ain't nothin' to worry about.'

Dehner looked at Max Chumley, whose face was expressionless, then replied, 'Well . . . OK.'

The three men crossed the street to a hitching rail where three horses were tied up. Sam approached the horse the closest to the light from the Lady Luck as it could be most easily seen. 'This here is the nag I was talkin' about.'

As Sam talked, he glanced upwards. Max Chumley drew his .45 and fired toward the roof of the Lady Luck. The bullet ricocheted near Sid Slocum, who rolled and then fired a shot, which burrowed into the ground near the lawmen. Chumley fired again, this time hitting his target in the shoulder, near the neck.

Dehner looked toward Sam Slocum, who was now lying on the boardwalk in front of the hitch rail. Sam started to draw his weapon but stopped as he saw the barrel of Dehner's Colt.

Another shot came from the rooftop. This time, both Dehner and Chumley returned fire. One of them sent a second bullet cutting into Sid Slocum. The killer realized he could be dying. He needed a doctor quick. He tossed the rifle off the roof and tried to stand with his hands up.

He didn't make it. The killer bent over and then fell off the roof, landing near his rifle. Chumley cautiously made his way toward the fallen gunman. That rifle was within easy reach.

As Sid Slocum's body plunged toward the ground, Dehner turned back to where Sid's brother had been lying. Sam was now on his feet and running across the street toward the saloon.

'Stop, Slocum, I'll shoot!'

Sam Slocum untied a horse in front of the Lady Luck. All of the shooting had spooked the chestnut, which neighed loudly and went up on its hind legs as Sam held on to the reins.

The horse blocked Dehner's chance for a good shot. Dehner took a fast glance at Max, who was crouched over the man who had fallen from the roof, then shouted at Sam Slocum.

'Give up, you haven't got a chance!'

Sam managed to mount the horse. He fired a shot at Dehner, which only terrified the chestnut more. The horse bucked and tried to throw its rider.

Dehner returned fire, a red spear ripped Sam Slocum's chest. Slocum hunched over the horn of the saddle and tried to fire again. Another bullet from Dehner's .45 flamed through the night and hit its target. Sam Slocum fell from the chestnut, which galloped off.

Dehner ran to Slocum; the outlaw was alive, but barely. As he crouched over the outlaw, Max ran to his side. 'Sid's dead. He broke his neck in the fall.'

Sam's voice was a weak whisper. 'I'll be joinin' him soon. Don't think the reunion is gonna be all that pleasant.'

'Who hired you, Sam?' Dehner asked.

The killer managed a slight laugh.

'Don't think it proper for a man to end his life by betrayin' a professional confidence.'

'Tell us who hired you.' Max's voice was a near shout. 'It's the decent thing to do, may help put you right with God.'

This time, Slocum's laugh was louder. 'A bit late for me to be worryin' about God's opinion. I'm gonna be spendin' my time with the other fella. Don't think ol' Beelzebub would be much impressed if I betrayed another crook. Might make him toss some extra coals on to the fire . . . '

Sam Slocum babbled a few more words and then went limp. As Dehner lifted the killer's wrist feeling for a pulse that wasn't there, he could hear footsteps fast approaching.

'What's goin' on?' Sheriff Amos Santell asked.

Dehner smiled whimsically as he stood up. 'Your deputy just saved my life, that's what is going on!' After giving the sheriff a quick account of what had happened, Dehner turned to Max Chumley. 'How did you figure one of the Slocums was going to ambush us from the roof?'

Max pushed his Stetson back off his forehead and began to rattle off facts like a boy reciting in school. 'Those fellers were mighty friendly to us earlier in the evening. Too friendly. Most saddlebums jus' don't act that way.'

'I should have thought of that,' Dehner said, 'but I didn't.'

Max continued. 'And Sam was mighty insistent that we not check the saloon for those hardcases he was jawing about. I figured the reason was 'cause there weren't no hardcases. I kept a close eye on that jasper when we crossed the street. He started looking up and I drew my gun.'

'You were wrong about one thing, Max,' Dehner said.

'What's that?'

'Earlier tonight, you told me you might not be cut out to be a lawman. Max, you were born to wear a star.'

'Dehner's right, Max. Yep, he is absolutely right.' There was a hint of an apology in the sheriff's voice.

'Thanks, Sheriff Santell. You saying that means a lot to me.' There was an awkward silence, then Max spoke again. 'I do have one favor to ask of you gents.'

'What's that?' Amos asked.

'Rod Baker, the newspaperman, will be asking about all that just happened,' Chumley explained. 'I jus' plan on giving him a few facts. Two saddlebums got outta hand and we had to kill them. No fancy stories 'bout me shooting an outlaw off the roof. Appreciate it if you gents would do the same. I've had it with being a hero.'

Both Dehner and the sheriff smiled and nodded in agreement.

★　★　★

Two hours later, Dehner, Amos Santell, and Max Chumley were sitting in the sheriff's office enjoying bad jokes and bad coffee. Dehner was pleased with the atmosphere that filled the office. The tension between Sheriff Santell and Deputy Chumley was completely gone.

After guffawing at one of his own lousy stories, the sheriff got up from behind his desk and ambled over to the coffee pot. He spoke as he poured himself another cup.

'This shooting tonight's got me confused.' He took a sip of coffee and looked at Dehner. 'The Slocum brothers were hired killers. But who hired them and who did they want to kill? You or Max, or both, and why?'

'Can't answer that question, Sheriff.' Dehner stared at the reflection that looked back at him from his coffee cup. His face bobbed about in a state of confusion. 'In fact, there are a lot of questions I can't answer.'

The detective got to his feet and began to wander about the office, coffee cup in hand. 'I got involved in this mess because I was tracking a hired gun, Curt Tatum. After killing Tatum, I learned that he was after Leona Carson, a girl of fourteen or so who hasn't got a dime to her name. Why would anyone pay a high-priced gunfighter to kill Leona?'

Amos Santell was still standing beside the coffee pot. 'Maybe the pappy of Leona's baby is one of the town's rich men. He's afraid the girl will tell the world what a sly dog he is and ruin his reputation.'

A dubious look creased Dehner's face. 'Could be. I've avoided questioning Leona about Samuel's father. Maybe that was a mistake, not that I think she would tell me. Still, I don't believe — '

'I don't believe so, either.' Max was slumped in one of two chairs that fronted the desk. 'Leona ain't said nothing about the boy's father. Besides, even if she did, a rich feller could jus' say Leona was lying. Most folks would probably believe him.'

Dehner stared into his coffee cup once again. His face still bobbed.

'Then, strange . . . crazy things kept happening. Reverend Jeremy Lanning was murdered by Ash Carrick, another expensive professional killer. Carrick posed as Lanning because that provided him with an opportunity to kill Leona. Then Carrick gets killed inside his jail cell.'

Chumley looked down at the floor. 'Nothing strange or crazy 'bout that. I just failed to check Carrick to see if he was carrying a knife.'

'Are you sure?'

Dehner's question surprised Chumley. 'What do you mean?'

'That lawyer, John Latchman, was being pretty forceful and belligerent for a man who had almost been murdered.' Dehner took a step toward Chumley. 'OK, you can't swear in court that you checked Ash Carrick carefully enough to find a small knife. But do you think you checked him carefully enough?'

Chumley paused but only for a moment. 'Yes, I do.'

Dehner fell silent as he began to walk

about the office. Santell gave the detective a curious look. 'Ya got somethin' on your mind, Rance?'

Rance Dehner pulled out his timepiece. The time was well after 3 a.m. 'It's a bit late now, but tomorrow I plan to call on a lady of the evening.'

18

June Day walked down the stairway to the first floor of the Lady Luck and realized she was in trouble. The owner of the saloon, George Hoffman, was at the bar and eyed her angrily as she made her descent.

George was talking with Fred, the bartender on duty. As June approached the bar, she tried to sound cheerful. 'A pretty good crowd for this early in the evening, looks like — '

'I need to talk to you.' The owner's voice was threatening.

'Sure, George.'

'Mr Hoffman! You call me Mr Hoffman, you cheap — ' George stepped toward her, his sunken, pockmarked face filling with rage.

'Of course, Mr Hoffman, if that's how you want it.'

The owner grabbed June by her wrist

and pulled her away from the bar. Hoffman enjoyed humiliating his girls in front of the customers. 'What happened last night?'

George Hoffman's face was now only inches from June's. The owner's rancid breath assaulted her. The woman tried to keep her emotions in check. 'If you mean those two Slocum brothers getting killed, I know nothing about it.'

'That's not what I'm talking about! What's the story on Jubal Collins? He's one of our regulars. He told me that last night you wouldn't go upstairs with him.'

A scattering of suppressed laughter sounded all around June. The patrons were enjoying the show as George chewed out one of his doves. The woman struggled to keep her speech from wavering. 'I arranged for Ellie to go upstairs with Jubal.'

'He didn't want Ellie! He wanted you!' George released the woman's wrist and slapped her across the face. 'There's a little reminder to start treating the customers right.'

June staggered backwards but managed to keep her balance. 'Don't you ever do that again . . . Mr Hoffman!'

Hoffman took a step toward her, his hand ready for another strike. 'I'll do whatever I want.'

Cheers, shouts, and laughter could be heard from the patrons, but not for long. A hard voice suddenly cut through the cacophony. 'Stop, right now!'

Dehner placed himself between June and her boss and gave Hoffman an intense stare. 'I don't like men who hit women.'

'You stay out of this! I'm George Hoffman and I own this place.' Hoffman couldn't back down in his own saloon surrounded by long-time customers.

Normally in a situation like this one, Dehner would try to give his opponent an out, a way to back out of a fight without losing face. But he had no interest in letting the owner of the Lady Luck save face. 'You're quite a tough guy, George. Why, I bet on a good day you could beat up the schoolmarm.'

Laughter screeched against the walls of the Lady Luck, but this time the crowd was mocking George Hoffman. Enraged, the saloon owner took a swing at Dehner, who ducked and countered with a roundhouse that sent Hoffman sprawling on to the floor of his own saloon.

Fred hurried from behind the bar to help his boss. The rest of the patrons began to return to their gambling and drinking. Dehner spoke in a low voice to June Day. 'I'd like to talk to you in private.'

June laughed good-naturedly. 'Sure. I guess I owe you.'

'That's not what I mean.'

'What do you mean?'

Dehner motioned her to the stairway. No one paid much heed as June Day walked upstairs with the deputy. After what had just happened, it seemed the natural thing to do.

She took him to a small room, which

was similar to the room where he and Amos Santell had stopped a skirmish between a saloon girl and a drifter. There was no chair, only a bed and a small chest of drawers. June walked toward the bed, turned and faced the lawman. 'You said you wanted to talk.'

'Yes, I've got a problem that maybe you can help me with.'

'Oh brother.'

Dehner took off his hat and began to pace the floor. 'Hear me out, would you?'

June sat down on the bed. 'Sure.'

Dehner stopped pacing and crossed his arms in front of his chest. 'Remember that run-in a few days ago with Tammy and a jasper called Wyoming?'

'Yes.'

'What do you know about Wyoming?'

'Never been there.'

'Come on, you know what I meant.'

June smirked. 'Sorry, in my job you get in the habit of making stupid remarks to stupid men who are boozed up enough to think you're clever.'

'Not all men are stupid, June.'

Dehner was surprised by June's reaction to his statement. The woman's face contorted and she looked away from him. 'I know, some men are nice, there are even some who are wonderful. Those men don't always get treated right, I . . . '

Dehner allowed June a few moments to compose herself, and then restated his question. 'What can you tell me about the guy who called himself Wyoming?'

'Everything and nothing.' June's voice was quiet and resigned. 'He was a type that passes through now and again. Probably a small-time crook between jobs. As you know, a lot of gangs pull a robbery, break up for a few months, then meet again for another go at it. I'd put Wyoming in that category.'

'How about Tammy?' Dehner asked. 'I've been looking around for her. She seems to have left town.'

This time the expression on June's face was one of curiosity. 'Yeah, Tammy left town all right.'

'I don't understand.'

'I didn't understand it myself,' June replied. 'But the day after that fracas with Wyoming, Tammy informed me that she was quitting her job and taking off. I asked her if she was going to England to attend a royal ball.'

'Why?'

'You should have seen the way she was dressed! All new clothes — expensive clothes!'

'Any idea where she got the money?'

A chagrinned look spread across June's face. 'I had my suspicions. I figured maybe Tammy was doing some work on her own outside of the Lady Luck. I didn't say anything. If George got wind of it he would have beaten Tammy, and me, too. I'm kind of in charge of the girls.'

'Looking back on it, do you still think that's how Tammy got the extra money?' Dehner asked.

'I don't know. If she did pull something like that she was very clever about it and Tammy was not the clever type. In fact, she was just plain stupid.'

Dehner ran a hand through his hair as if trying to rattle loose some ideas. 'I'm beginning to think that the whole Wyoming-Tammy dust-up was a big show, a distraction to get Sheriff Santell and me away from the jailhouse while Ash Carrick was being shot.'

The detective stared at a wall for a moment. He tugged at an ear lobe as he looked back at June. 'Do you know a lawyer here in town named John Latchman?'

A vague expression played on the woman's face. 'Yes, sort of. I know who you mean. Gambles some at the Lady Luck . . . doesn't spend much money on the girls . . . what day is it?'

'Monday.'

'He may stop by the saloon tomorrow afternoon. On Tuesdays he closes his office at noon and often stops by here for a quick drink. We have two barkeeps: Fred and Larry. He enjoys jawing with Larry, but if Fred's behind the bar, he'll talk with me or one of the other girls. He doesn't stay long.'

'Why does he close his office at noon on Tuesdays?'

The woman shrugged her shoulders. 'How should I know? Maybe he wants to read the Good Book to get ready for Wednesday night prayer meeting.'

'Was Latchman hanging around the saloon much on the days right before Tammy and Wyoming had their spat, or maybe on the day itself?'

The vagueness remained in June's eyes. 'Maybe. He might have been there on that day. I recall seeing a very well-dressed gent — could have been Latchman.' The woman laughed bitterly. 'You know there's not much difference between a well-dressed gentleman and a dusty cow-poke. They're all fools, expecting you to treat them like kings.'

Dehner stared at his hat as he shifted it from one hand to another. 'Can't think of any more questions. Thank you, I'll — '

June was crying, silently but uncontrollably. Dehner let her alone for a few moments then crouched down beside her. 'I always seem to have this effect on women.'

June managed a laugh, which was a partial sob. 'It's not you. It's me. I've been jabbering on about how awful men are and how Tammy's stupid. Let me tell you, no one is more stupid than me. I had a wonderful husband and I ran out on him for . . . '

The woman went back to her crying. Dehner moved up out of his crouch. He waited until the woman's crying had subsided, then placed some money on the bed beside her.

June eyed the bills and anger shot from her eyes. 'What's that for?'

'A ticket.'

The anger was replaced by confusion. 'A ticket to where?'

'Wherever that husband of yours is.'

June inhaled and placed a hand against her chest. 'I couldn't do that. I can't go back. He'd throw me out. He has every right to. I'd make a fool of myself — '

'I suppose you're real proud of the

life you have now.'

'No . . . but — '

'Go back and try to rebuild what you destroyed. Even if you fail, you'll know that you tried to set things right. That's a lot better than going through life hating yourself.'

Dehner paused. He could think of nothing more to say. 'The decision is yours, June.'

He walked quietly out the door. Before closing it he looked back. June was staring at the money beside her.

19

The detective guided his horse into a grove of trees and pulled field glasses from his saddle-bag. John Latchman was riding at a brisk trot toward what appeared to be an old, long-abandoned ranch house.

Yesterday, June Day had told Dehner that the lawyer always took Tuesday afternoons off. She couldn't answer his question as to why. Dehner was about to get the answer himself.

Latchman rode to the back of the house. He did not appear after several minutes.

'The man must have entered the place through a back door,' Dehner said to his bay as he gave the animal a pat. 'We detectives are trained to figure out such complex problems.'

He dismounted and tethered his horse to a cottonwood. He moved quietly to the back of the house and a densely forested area. In a small clearing in that forest, near the house, two horses were tied up. The people inside obviously don't want anyone to know they are here, Dehner thought.

He moved to the side of the house and a small window. Two voices could be heard. The first obviously belonged to John Latchman.

'Rose, seeing you once a week isn't enough. Leave that old man. Yes, people will gossip. Let them! We'll make a great life together, just — '

'You know that's what I want, John. And we'll have it. But we have to move slowly. And we don't have much time today. My brother's coming in on the stage. Everything's going to work out the way we planned. Be patient.'

Latchman's voice took on a playful quality. 'I'm not feeling very patient right now.'

Rose Whitney began to laugh. Dehner had heard enough.

Riding back to Hardin, the detective felt low and uncomfortable as if a layer of dirt had settled on him, which would never wash off. He thought about his year with Pinkerton, listening to his colleagues guffaw over stories about cheating wives and wayward husbands. Snooping through the wreckages of failed marriages was not his idea of being a detective. And he didn't want to work with men who enjoyed wallowing in filthy mud.

Dehner put such thoughts aside and began to speculate as to whether he had just discovered anything important. John Latchman was having an affair with Rose Whitney. For reasons he himself did not completely understand, Dehner decided to keep that information confidential for the time being.

There was one element to all of this that struck him as being very important. Rose Whitney was the one controlling the situation. She obviously had John Latchman marching to her orders.

The afternoon was hot, but that thought sent a cold shudder through the detective.

20

As the stagecoach approached Hardin, Texas, Bradford Maltin felt uneasy. He hadn't spoken to his son Will during the whole trip from San Antonio. Bradford spit tobacco particles out the window and decided it didn't really matter. He had no interest in anything his son had to say.

Inhaling on his large cigar, the businessman realized that wasn't quite true. One matter concerning his son did interest him. But he couldn't discuss it here. There was a third passenger in the stagecoach; a well dressed, pudgy man with a constant smile.

That smile is grotesque, Bradford thought to himself. The man is obviously a drummer and not a successful one. His desperation is as apparent as his yellow, crooked teeth.

Bradford realized that if he spoke a

word the drummer would jump in with a pile of inane prattle. Of course, his jawing would eventually become a sales pitch.

When the stagecoach arrived at Hardin, Bradford Maltin was the first out. He retrieved the two cowhide valises belonging to him and Will, and then set them down on the boardwalk and smiled as a familiar face approached.

'Sheriff Santell.' Anyone hearing Bradford's voice would have thought his good cheer genuine. 'I see that lawmen still greet the stage when it pulls into Hardin.'

Santell shook hands with both the businessman and his son. 'Good to have ya and Will back in town, Mr Maltin. Will comes to visit quite a bit but it's been, what, 'bout three years since ya've been here?'

'At least,' the businessman replied.

The sheriff nodded toward the man standing beside him. 'This here gent is serving as a deputy for a spell: Rance Dehner.'

'Pleased to meet you, Mr Maltin. I've already met Will,' Dehner spoke as he also shook hands with the two new arrivals. 'Will you gentlemen be staying out at the Whitney ranch?'

'No.' Bradford's smile widened. 'Will and I will be staying at the hotel. Don't want to be a burden on my little sister and her husband. Remember what Ben Franklin said: 'Fish and guests begin to smell after three days'.'

Everyone except Will laughed. There was some more bantering between Bradford Maltin and the lawmen. As they talked, Dehner noticed that Bradford Maltin was in remarkably good physical shape for a man who spent most of his working days behind a desk. Dehner reckoned he must be an avid hunter or had another hobby that kept him physically active. The businessman's face was also youthful. There were only a few lines there. His hair was black, thick, and contained no gray.

What interested the detective the most was Will Maltin. Will stood behind his father saying nothing and looking like he wanted to disappear.

When the lawmen left to continue on their rounds, the good-natured cheer vanished from Bradford Maltin. He hastily walked back to the valises, picked one up, and gestured for Will to take the other.

The drummer was still standing around outside the stage depot. He approached the two Maltins anxiously. 'It was a pleasure travelling with you gentlemen. We never did introduce ourselves. My name is . . . '

Bradford hurried by the drummer, his son trailing after him. The businessman moved at a fast pace down the boardwalk and almost charged through the hotel doors, which were open.

He moved in a direct line to the hotel's wide counter where a clerk with a wide girth and a wide smile greeted him. 'Afternoon, sir!'

'I'll take a room.' Bradford glanced at his son who looked sheepish and completely absorbed in his own thoughts.

The businessman realized he wanted to spend as little time with Will as possible. 'Make that two rooms.'

'Yes sir.' The desk clerk retrieved two keys from the cubby holes behind him.

'I'll be needing a horse.' Bradford was half talking to himself and half addressing the clerk.

'The place you want to go is right down the street. Riley's Blacksmith and Livery, owned by — '

'By Horace Riley!' Bradford snapped as if the desk clerk had just insulted him. 'I remember Horace from my last trip to this . . . town.' He turned to his son. 'Come on!'

The rooms were both on the second floor. They arrived at Bradford's room first. 'Come in,' the businessman ordered his son. 'We have to talk.'

Inside, the room was a bit nicer than what might be expected for a small town like Hardin, but Bradford didn't notice. He put his valise down beside the bed, made a fist with his right hand and slammed it into his left palm.

'Nothing's going right.' He seemed to be addressing the gods, informing them that they were falling down on the job.

He paused for a few moments, then gave up on the gods and addressed his son. 'Let's start from the beginning. How'd you meet this Lena?'

'Leona.' Will dropped his valise on to the floor.

'Leona! How'd you meet her?'

'Last spring when I was on one of my visits to Aunt Rose and Uncle Earl — '

'Yes, yes, how'd you meet the girl?'

'Sometimes I'd come into town by myself on Saturday night. Leona was a waitress at the restaurant.'

Bradford's voice dripped with sarcasm. 'And you two became right cordial.'

'One night we took a walk and stopped under a tree outside of town.'

'OK, OK. When did you find out she was pregnant?'

'Four months later, I visited Hardin again. Leona was showing. She told me I was the baby's father but I didn't have to marry her if I didn't want to. She had kept it a secret about me being the father. I was scared. I didn't know what to do.'

'And you didn't tell anyone at all?'

Will had seen the look of disgust on his father's face when he had used the word, 'scared.' His voice became heavy with shame. 'No. I told no one.'

Bradford had no interest in his son's mood. He continued with the questions. 'When the baby was born Leona sent you that letter. The one I found.'

'Yes. The baby was a boy. She named it Samuel.'

'I know that!'

Bradford looked about the room hurriedly, and for the first time noticed it was well kept and had an ashtray on a table beside the bed. He crushed the remaining stub of his cigar into the tray in a gesture of anger. 'Samuel is mine. I've wasted too much time and money on this. At least I didn't give Curt Tatum the whole thousand up front.'

Will's eyes flamed as he began to

understand his father's words. 'Did you hire Curt Tatum to get Samuel?'

'Yes.' The older man was consumed by private thoughts as he plotted his next move.

'What was Tatum supposed to do about Leona?' Will's voice sounded incredulous.

His father didn't notice. 'Kill her. She could have caused trouble. Wasn't worth taking a chance. Tatum was supposed to take the baby to the Whitney ranch. Rose and I had a story ready. Rose would have kept Samuel until your mother and I came for the baby. Your mother would have believed the cockeyed story Rose and I came up with. She would love another child.'

Will Bradford's heart began to beat faster and he felt faint. He had always cherished the times he spent with his aunt and uncle. Their ranch was a special place for him. But there was nothing special about it after all; the Whitney ranch was just a branch office of his father's operations.

The young man inhaled deeply as if to maintain consciousness. His father had talked so casually about killing Leona, as if ordering her dead was like squashing one of his burnt-out cigars.

'Why?!' Will's voice sounded like something between a shout and a sob. 'Why kill Leona? She never hurt you.'

Bradford took a few steps toward his son, then back handed him viciously across the face. The young man stumbled, just barely staying on his feet.

'I'll tell you why.' Bradford spoke in a low rumble. 'Because your older brother died rescuing you from drowning. You're worthless. You might as well have been a girl. Your mother and I can't have any more kids. I've worked like a dog all my life, and I want someone to leave my property to. I need a grandson. Samuel may be a stray, but he's still my flesh and blood.'

Will slurred his words a little, his father's assault still ringing in his head. 'I'll marry someday, h-have ch-children.'

'Do you think I want some kid you

raised? No! I was close to your brother, but not you, and look what happened. I'm going to raise Samuel. He'll be a man, not worthless like you.'

Will was beginning to regain his balance and his speech. 'You hate me.'

The statement seemed to make his father a bit whimsical. 'Not really. There's nothing to hate about you, Will, you're just a weakling. Don't worry. I'll send you money whenever you need it. You can visit us whenever you want. We'll have us some real nice family get togethers.'

Bradford chuckled lightly; he seemed genuinely amused. Will's body trembled.

'Go to your room and stay there.' The amusement was gone from the older man's voice. 'I brought you along because I thought I might need you. Right now, that's not the case. Take supper in the dining room downstairs. I'm going out to the ranch, I'll tell them you got sick on the ride here.'

Will desperately wanted to disobey his father, or at least make a cutting remark as he left. He did none of that. He picked up his valise and walked out of the room, gently closing the door behind him.

Bradford lit another cigar, remembering his doctor's advice to cut back on the stogies. As he exhaled a cloud of smoke, the businessman mused on the fact that he did what he pleased and got what he wanted. Getting to this point in life had been hard but he intended to savor his wealth and status for all it was worth.

There was only one thing he lacked — an heir. A man who someday would be strong enough to take over the empire he was building. Samuel would become that man and nothing would stop Bradford Maltin from making that desire come true.

21

Bradford leaned against the large corral at the Whitney ranch. His sister was beside him. Any onlooker would think they were admiring the horses while indulging in brother/sister chitchat.

'How much money do you need?' Bradford's voice sounded incredulous.

'You heard what I said.' Rose smiled sweetly and waved at a ranch-hand who was a safe distance away. 'Look, I read the mail and do the books for Earl. He hates that kind of thing. But I can't move money around forever. The money I spent must be replaced.'

'I didn't tell you to spend that much!'

'Yes you did, big brother, in that letter you sent instructing to me to kill Leona and get Samuel.'

Bradford drummed his fingers against the corral. 'This Ash Carrick, he was recommended by one of the contacts you retained from your, ah, former line of work?'

Rose smirked and nodded her head. 'I made the arrangements during our last trip to San Antonio. Remember? Earl and I went there to talk with a bishop of the Methodist Church about sending Hardin a new pastor. While Earl socialized with some old army buddies I got together with a . . . friend, who recommended Ash Carrick.'

'Having Carrick kill the preacher was your idea?'

'And it would have worked if not for that Dehner fellow.'

'The same man who killed Curt Tatum?'

'Yes!' Rose made a fist as if getting ready to punch Rance Dehner. 'And he remains a dangerous man. Like I told you, he's determined to find out who's trying to kill Leona and why. That's why I hired the Slocum brothers to get rid of him.'

'You used the same contact to hire the Slocums?'

'The same. He passed through Hardin wanting to find out what happened to Carrick.' Rose laughed bitterly. 'So far, he hasn't shown up inquiring as to what happened to the Slocums.'

'You have Leona right here at the ranch, did you ever think about — '

'No! That can't happen! If Leona were to be killed here there would be an investigation, I might become a suspect, Dehner would — '

'Of course, of course.' Bradford waved a hand back and forth as if erasing his previous notion. 'There should be no more attempts on Leona's life here in Hardin. That's why I am taking her back to San Antonio where she can meet with an unfortunate accident.'

'Better wait for a decent interval. Dehner will — '

'I have it all thought out. What are some of Leona's interests?'

The question surprised Rose. 'Ah . . . she's very good with her hands. Plays the piano well, for someone who has never had any training. She has made a carrier for Samuel so she can carry him on her back, the way an Indian woman would carry a baby.'

Bradford gave his sister a crooked smile. 'And that lawyer friend of yours that you wrote me about. He will be here tonight and back up anything I say with legal mumbo jumbo?'

'John Latchman will be here and he will do anything I ask. He has already killed for me.'

Bradford's smile became one of admiration for his sister. He felt a real bond with her, a bond he could feel for no one else. They had both been born poor and now were rich. The climb had been hard and neither one of them had played by the rules. But rules were for timid people, those who were content with just getting by. Bradford Maltin wasn't timid and neither was his sister. Rose was wealthy and successful. Money and success. That was all that mattered.

22

Leona sat in the living room with her hands folded in her lap, trying to appear calm. She wanted to be in the kitchen helping Esther clean up the dinner dishes, not being smiled at by four people.

Two of the four were men she had just met at dinner: Bradford Maltin, Will's father and Rose's brother; and John Latchman, a lawyer she had seen in town several times but never actually met. The other two were Rose and Earl. Earl was the only person present Leona felt comfortable with and she thought he didn't appear all that happy with what was going on.

His entire body seemed to twitch as he sat on a sofa with his wife, who, as always, seemed perfectly composed. Maltin and Latchman were both on their feet though there were chairs available to them.

Bradford Maltin was surprised by the sudden nervousness that gripped him as he began to speak to the girl. 'Leona, my son Will has told me . . . well, he has told me everything. I want to help you . . . ah . . . help you have a good life. You and Samuel.'

'Thank you, sir.' Leona tried to hold her smile. 'But Samuel and me will get along. You don't need to do anythin' for us.'

'But I want to do something!' Bradford's voice boomed. 'I understand you play a mean piano and you're very good at craft work.'

Leona glanced nervously at Rose and Earl, then looked back at Bradford. 'Thank you for sayin' so, sir.'

Bradford continued. 'You know, the Bible says that it is wrong for us to hide our candle under a bushel.' He had heard that quote many times over the years. He was reasonably sure it came from the Bible.

'Yes sir, I try to read the Good Book ever' day.'

219

'Wonderful!' Bradford thought he saw a slight cringe move across his sister's face. Maybe he should have allowed Rose to handle this. Making a persuasive argument to a girl in her early teenage years was not a skill he had needed to hone.

The businessman pressed on. 'I have enrolled you in the Stanbury School for Young Ladies in San Antonio. There you will receive a fine education — '

'But, sir, what about Samuel?'

Bradford held up an index finger indicating he had everything well in hand. 'I have taken a room for you and Samuel at a boarding house near the school and arranged for someone to look after the baby while you are in class.'

Leona began to wring her hands. 'I appreciate all you've done, sir — '

'This is a marvelous opportunity for you, Leona.' Latchman's smile was less broad than Bradford's and his voice more officious. 'Mr Maltin has been extraordinarily generous. I have examined the papers myself. Bradford Maltin has arranged to pay all of your expenses.

You are a very fortunate young woman.'

The skin around Leona's mouth seemed to tighten. 'Obliged.'

'We will leave for San Antonio tomorrow,' Bradford declared.

'Tomorrow!' Alarm sounded in the young woman's voice.

Earl Whitney gave Bradford an incredulous look. 'Now, hold on, Bradford! Don't you think Leona should be given a chance to think this over?'

Rose placed a calming hand on her husband's shoulder. 'What is there to think over, Earl? Leona may be a bit overwhelmed now, but if she doesn't take Bradford's offer, why, she'd never forgive herself when she got older.'

'I guess you're right.' Earl looked directly at Leona. 'This is a fine opportunity for you.'

The young woman had just lost her only potential ally. She looked at no one in particular as she spoke. 'Thanks, appreciate what you're doin' for me. Would it be OK if I went outside and took a little walk around the ranch, maybe ride one of the horses a bit, this bein' my last night here and all?'

'Well, I see no reason why not,' Rose said. 'You go right ahead, Leona.'

After the girl stepped outside, Bradford turned to his sister. The forced good humor was gone from his voice. 'You don't think she'll run off do you?'

Rose could tell from the expression on her husband's face that he had caught the harsh undertone in her brother's voice. She beamed a bright smile as she arose from the sofa and put a hand on Bradford's shoulder. Her voice sounded comforting as if reassuring Bradford in regard to a girl he was trying to help.

'Don't worry, dear, Leona won't run off with Samuel here at the ranch house. She just has a lot to think about right now.' Rose squeezed her brother's arm and looked him directly in the eye.

'There is nothing to worry about,' she said.

★   ★   ★

Leona Carson held an old timepiece in her hand. She had found it in the top drawer of the large chest of drawers in the guest room of the Whitney ranch. Immediately after finding it, she had shown the yellow object to Earl Whitney, who laughed at it.

'I had wondered what happened to that thing.' He wound the timepiece and set the time. 'Why, it still works!' He handed it back to Leona. 'You can use it to tell time, if you don't mind peering around the crack in the glass.'

Leona didn't mind. She walked to the window of the guest room in order to take advantage of the moonlight. She needed to be cautious. Unlikely as it would be at this late hour, someone might notice the light seeping under the doorway if she lit the lamp in the room.

Leona pressed her lips together as she checked the time. It was close to 1.30 a.m.; time to make her move. The young woman took a few quiet steps toward the bed. Samuel was sleeping. She gently lifted him and placed him in the carrier, which she strapped to her back.

The young mother walked around the room allowing Samuel to adjust to the movement. She recalled the good-natured kidding she had received from the ranch-hands when they spotted Samuel strapped to her back a few days before. They had called her the Indian maiden. Well, in her opinion, those Indian maidens were pretty smart.

Samuel continued to sleep soundly. Leona opened the window, which was large enough for her to crawl through while carrying the baby.

Outside, Leona Carson made her way quietly toward the barn. The moonlight was now a problem; she and Samuel were creating a silhouette. The young woman was especially cautious as she made her way past the bunkhouse. Leona got along well with the ranch-hands but they'd stop her if they spotted her running off.

She made her way stealthily around the barn. The horse was there, saddled and ready. Leona had prepared the horse several hours before when she told everyone she wanted to take 'a little walk around the ranch, maybe ride one of the horses'. Leona knew she couldn't have gone into the barn and saddled the horse this late at night — too much noise.

The young woman took the reins of the buckskin and quietly walked it far away from the ranch house. Then, fear and excitement coursing through her veins, she mounted and galloped off.

23

Del Burgess awoke from a nightmare. Horrifying images popped and vanished like soap bubbles as he heard a horse on the runway of Riley's Blacksmith and Livery. He sprang up, brushed the straw off his body, and hustled outside of the stall where he had been sleeping. Del needed to get to the customer before the guy called out, 'Anyone here?' or a similar shout, which could wake his boss. Horace Riley didn't enjoy being roused from his sleep.

Del quickly lit the lantern that hung on the stall and began to make his way to the runway. He was stunned when he saw Leona walking briskly toward him. She looked terrified. He embraced the young woman but not tightly. Samuel was strapped to her back and he had the lantern in his hand.

'What's wrong?' Del asked as he released her.

'Bradford Maltin, Will's father, he wants to take me to San Antonio, put me in a school of some kind.'

'What! He can't make you do something like that against your will.'

'Yes, he can, Del! He's got money, power and ain't no one talkin' back to him. I'm suppose ta leave with him tomorra.'

'Tomorrow . . . ' Del sifted through the many half thoughts stampeding through his mind. 'Leona, I done told you how I feel. I love you. I want to marry you and be a father to Samuel.'

Hope began to crowd the fear from Leona's face. 'Yes.'

'Well, now's the time. We'll ride to Akin tonight, find a preacher to marry us, then head out for California, make a life for ourselves there.'

'Del, that's a wonderful idea,' Leona said.

'No, it ain't!'

Horace Riley's loud voice woke up Samuel, who began to cry. Leona hastily unstrapped the baby and began to cradle him in her arms as Horace stepped into the lantern light.

Del smiled lamely at his boss. 'Mr Riley, how long — '

'I heard ever' thing ya said. Can't say I blame ya for running off. I'd do the same in your shoes.'

Leona rocked the baby as she spoke. 'But you just said — '

'I meant going to Akin was a fool idea,' Horace explained.

Del looked confused. 'But Akin is the nearest town.'

'Yeah, and it's the first place that rich man Maltin and his friends will come looking for ya. Besides, have ya been in Akin lately?'

Both young people shook their heads.

'The place is dying,' Horace declared. 'I doubt if they even got them a preacher anymore. The place ya need to go is Prentiss.'

Del's eyes narrowed. 'That's a lot further ride.'

'Yeah,' Horace acknowledged. 'But the road is smoother and ya got a bright moon and stars to help ya along. B'sides, sunup ain't that far away. And there's a lot happening in Prentiss. Ya can work there for a spell and get some coins to put in your pocket 'fore ya head out to Caleefornya.'

Samuel had stopped crying and Leona held him against her shoulder. 'We can't stay there too long. Bradford Maltin will find us.'

Horace laughed, sending out a spray of brown saliva. 'I'll fix that.'

The laugh startled Samuel, who began to cry again. Leona began to pat the baby. 'How?'

'Like I said, Akin is the first place Maltin will look for ya. Well, I got me a friend in Akin. A bartender. He owes me a few favors . . . to be honest, a lot more than a few. I'll tell him to tell Bradford Maltin that you and Del stopped by Akin and jawed about going to Houston. That should keep Bradford off your trail for a spell.'

'Thanks, Mr Riley.' Del inhaled nervously, and then continued. 'Think maybe you could let us have two fresh horses? We'll send you the money from Prentiss.'

'I'll do better than that, though ya won't need to send me nothing. I want ya to take that small buckboard of mine and two strong horses. What with a baby and all, you'll need a buckboard to get ya to Caleefornya.'

Del shook his head vigorously. 'I can't let you do that, Mr Riley. I know how tight your money is right now.'

Horace waved both of his arms upwards. 'My money is always tight. That is, when I got any at all. Say, what's wrong with ya, girl?'

Tears were coursing across Leona's cheeks. 'Mr Riley, I've never thought of you as being a kind man because you never pay Del much and . . . well . . . Del felt that he had to wait until you had a few drinks before he asked if I could stay here and — '

'And I'm a loud-mouth who complains when things don't go his way which is jus' 'bout always.' This time Horace's laugh was softer with no accompanying spray. 'Well, even a gruff ol' son of a . . . gun . . . like me can do something decent now and again. Enough talk! We gotta git ya on your way!'

Horace led them outside to the back of the livery where stood a corral and three buckboards the blacksmith rented out. He and Del retrieved two horses from the corral and hitched them to one of the buckboards. When they were finished, Horace patted the wagon in an almost affectionate manner. 'This honey is almost new. It'll git ya to Prentiss and then to Calefornya jus' fine. Now, I want ya to wait here. I'll be right back.'

The huge man disappeared into the livery then emerged carrying a rifle and a small box with a thick string tied over it. 'This ol' Henry look familiar to ya, Del?'

'Sure, you loaned it to me once. I did some hunting. Brought us back some rabbits.'

'I want ya to have it.' Horace handed the young man the rifle and the box. 'It ain't loaded, so I gave ya the box of ammo. Rabbit meat might taste good on the way to Caleefornya. And, ya never know, ya might need it to protect yourself.'

This time, a tear or two were unleashed from Del's eyes. 'Thanks, Mr Riley. I'll never forget you.'

'I won't either,' Leona said as she strapped the carrier around her. Samuel was once again sleeping inside. 'I'll write you when we get to California. I hope we see you again someday, I know we'll see you in heaven.' She stood on her toes and gave Horace a kiss on his cheek.

The blacksmith smiled. 'Time for both of ya to get going before I start blubbering. The road here behind the buildings is wide; stay on it to ya git to the edge of town. The fewer folks that see ya, the better.'

Horace waved cheerfully at the departing buckboard. As the wagon turned and disappeared, he gently caressed the cheek that Leona had kissed, feeling the warm moisture there. She was a fine gal, he thought. They were both nice kids.

For a moment he experienced a pang of guilt and thought about not going through with his plan, but only for a moment. 'This is a tough, brutal world,' he said aloud. 'A man's gotta grab every chance he has.'

His voice sounded hard and cold.

24

'What do you want?' Bradford Maltin stood in the doorway of his hotel room, anger on his unshaven face.

'Sorry to wake ya, Mr Maltin,' Horace Riley said. 'But ya need to know something, something about Leona Carson.'

Maltin's anger turned to intense interest. 'Come in.' He closed the door behind the blacksmith.

Riley began to relate the story of Leona's late night trip to the livery as Bradford tossed off his robe and began to dress. At first, he appeared confused by the account. 'Couldn't you have stalled them? Got them to stay in town at least until sunup?'

'No. They was determined to leave. But I did trick 'em some.'

'What do you mean?' Bradford spoke as he tucked in his shirt.

'They planned on going to Akin. I

talked 'em into going to Prentiss. That's farther away and the road there is wide. And I gave them a small buckboard. They'll travel slower and their trail will be easy to follow.'

Bradford smiled as he sat on the bed and began to put on his socks. 'You've handled the situation very well, Horace.'

'Thanks, Mr Maltin.' Horace's tongue ran nervously across the top of his mouth, his words ran together as he spoke. 'Ya know, Mr Maltin, I've got my whole life put in that livery of mine. Ya being a businessman yourself I know ya understand. But, I've got some big problems with the bank. I could lose everything . . . '

Bradford listened almost joyfully to the blacksmith's words as he slipped on his boots. Horace Riley was a man desperate for money, meaning he was totally under Bradford's control.

He stood up and placed a hand on Riley's shoulder. 'Don't worry about a thing, Horace. Once we get Leona back, I'll buy you breakfast and you can tell me what you need.'

'Thanks, Mr Maltin, I — '

'You know this area a lot better than I do, Horace.' The businessman reached into his valise, which lay on the floor beside the bed. He pulled out a shoulder holster and put it on. He slipped on a jacket, which covered the weapon. 'I'm depending on you to lead me to those runaways.'

Horace quickly changed back into the no-nonsense man of action; the man who would be an invaluable help to Bradford Maltin. 'Yes sir, Mr Maltin. Let's get us over to the livery, quick. I got two fresh horses, saddled and waiting.'

Bradford and Horace left the hotel room and headed for the stairway. They didn't notice the door to the room next door opening and then closing slowly so as not to make a sound.

* * *

The two men walked briskly into the livery, and Horace lit two lanterns that hung on each side of the doorway. There was still a need for kerosene light, though dawn was beginning to repel the night. Maltin spotted an old man sleeping on a bed of straw several yards away. 'Who's that?'

'Jeffords,' Horace replied, 'the swamper at the Lady Luck. He does some work for me now and again. Caught him leaving work 'fore I came to git ya. Don't wanna leave this place with no — '

Bradford began looking around. 'I see you keep some rifles here.'

Horace gave the businessman a slightly comical salute. 'Yes sir. Got two fine Winchesters, all loaded.'

There was nothing comical in Bradford's voice. 'We may need them.'

Horace nodded his head and quickly retrieved the rifles from the rack on the wall. He handed one to Bradford. 'I put a box of ammo in our saddle-bags.'

Bradford smiled approvingly. 'You've thought of everything, Horace. Once we catch up with them, I'm hoping that Leona and Del will come to their senses. But they may not. We may have to take some . . . well . . . things may get unpleasant. I'm counting on you to, let's say, show discernment.'

Horace nodded again. 'I understand.'

Bradford looked at the gun in his hands intently, and then his eyes once again went to the blacksmith. 'I think we should get Latchman, the lawyer, to come with us.'

'You and me can handle it, Mr Maltin.'

'Yes, but having a lawyer with us makes it all look more legitimate. We were trying to stop Leona from running off for legal reasons. Samuel is my grandson and I was asserting my legal rights to — '

'That's right, Father! Put a nice and proper façade on all the evil you do!'

Will Maltin had shouted those words from the open doorway of the livery. His face was red as he approached his father. 'Kill anyone you want! Even a girl who's done you no harm!'

Bradford turned and faced his son.

'Get back to your room.'

Will began to breathe heavily as if the process was a struggle. 'I'm not a child anymore. You can't order me to my room. No, Father, I'm not going away and you are not going to hurt Leona.'

'And how are you going to stop me?' An element of curiosity invaded Bradford's voice. He was strongly interested in the answer to his question.

Will sensed that interest but fumbled for a response. 'I'll . . . well . . . I'll go to the sheriff. Yes, that's it. There's law in this town and you told me you hired Curt Tatum. I'll tell the sheriff. He'll have you arrested for — '

In one fast, brutal move, Bradford Maltin raised his Winchester in both hands and slammed it into the side of his son's head. Will gave a short, high-pitched squeal and collapsed.

Bradford looked down on his son's body. The businessman's face reflected mourning, as if a fragile hope lay in ruins before him.

Horace spoke in a whisper. 'I can

wake Jeffords. Have him git the boy to the doc. The doctor is usta being woke up — '

'Forget it.' Bradford spoke in a monotone, yet his voice seemed to come from the deepest pit of hell. 'My son isn't worth losing sleep over. Let's ride.'

25

Rance Dehner stepped out of the jail area and into the sheriff's office. He was accompanied by Max Chumley, Amos Santell and Doctor Patrick Curry. Once the door to the jail cells was closed, all four men began to laugh.

'Let this be a lesson to ya, Deputy,' Amos spoke between guffaws. 'No matter how old a lawdog may be, he's still got a lot to learn. I really thought it was OK to put them four drunks in the same cell together.'

'Max isn't just a deputy. He's also a prophet.' Dehner rubbed his shin bone where he had absorbed a kick about thirty minutes earlier. 'He predicted those four jaspers would get into a fight bigger than the one they pulled off at the Lady Luck.'

'My prophesying ain't all that good. I didn't think one of them would bite part of another's ear off. Tell me, Doc, the guy who lost a chunk of his ear. Is that gonna hurt his hearing any?'

The doctor's smile was tired but genuine. 'It sure won't help it.'

There was a round of laughter, which Amos Santell concluded with an offer. 'Care for a cup of coffee, Doc?'

'No thanks.' The doctor pulled a timepiece from his pocket. 'It's after half past four. I have to leave for the Smith ranch in about an hour. I'm going to see if I can grab a catnap first.'

The doctor waved to the three men and departed. Santell stepped out of the office, shouted a 'Thanks again, Doc,' and then returned inside.

'We've got those jaspers settled down now,' Dehner said. 'I'll do a round, give you two gents a little time for coffee.'

'Obliged,' the sheriff replied.

Dehner hesitated and then tried to speak in a casual voice. 'I do have a suggestion to make . . . ah . . . regarding our rounds.'

'What might that be?' Chumley asked

as he poured a cup of java.

'For the next few days or so, go by John Latchman's house and office on every round. Don't let the lawyer know what you're doing but keep an eye on that man.'

Both the sheriff and his deputy were surprised by Dehner's suggestion. Santell's eyes became probing. 'Ya got any purposes behind this notion, Rance?

'Yes, but I'd prefer not to go into details right now.'

Santell's eyes became more probing but the sheriff's hand waved nonchalantly in front of his face. 'Sure. But I'll be expecting ya to give me some of them details before I see too many more sunrises.'

'OK, Sheriff.' Dehner gave a two-fingered salute and left.

Outside, the detective began to walk slowly down the boardwalk. Streaks of red were invading the sky. Time to rouse the saddlebums, who were sleeping it off in the alley beside the saloon.

Dehner heard hoof beats coming

from the back road behind the buildings across the street. That back road received good use during the day. Stores used it for deliveries, leaving the main road unblocked.

The detective advanced down the boardwalk, staying in range of the hoof beats. It was a bit early for deliveries and, besides, there were no sounds of a wagon, just two horses.

At the end of the street, the riders emerged from the back road. Dehner pressed his body against the Lady Luck and watched. The two horsemen formed a dark silhouette and the detective couldn't be sure as to their identities. But he was very intrigued by the direction in which they were riding.

* * *

Bradford Maltin and Horace Riley pulled up in front of a small but well cared-for house with a white picket fence. Bradford looked the place over carefully as if the house gave him a deeper insight into the man who resided inside.

'So this is the home of Hardin's only barrister?'

There was something in the tone of his voice that made Horace uneasy. 'Ah . . . yes sir.'

'I'll only be a moment.' Bradford hastily dismounted, opened the gate of the fence, and almost ran up the path to the porch. He gave the front door several hard knocks.

The door opened revealing John Latchman in bare feet, wearing a robe with a gun in his right hand. 'Bradford?'

Maltin pushed the lawyer back into his house and closed the door. 'My, my, Counselor, greeting visitors to your home with a gun. Looks like committing murder has given you an uneasy conscience.'

'Ash Carrick deserved to die.'

'Probably. I don't care. Get dressed fast. You're riding with Horace Riley and me.'

'Why?'

Anger flared in Bradford's face and voice. 'Why? Because a nobody named Del Burgess and some cheap tramp are running off with my grandson! Those two fools are going to die this morning. My grandson will take his rightful place.'

'Sure, Bradford, but you don't need me for that.'

'I just might. Horace Riley's word may not mean much. He's a loud mouth and he's in way over his head with the bank.' Bradford gave a cynical laugh. 'I need the testimony of a prominent citizen such as yourself. You can come up with a good story bathed in legal mumbo jumbo.'

'I don't know, I — '

Maltin grabbed the lawyer by the lapels of his robe. 'You listen to me, Counselor. You've already murdered one man. There's no turning back. If you are going to have a life worth anything you are going to have to be hard. There are two kinds of people in this world: successes and failures.

Which are you?'

Latchman's voice quivered but he managed to say, 'A success.'

'That's just fine. But to get what you want and to keep it, you're going to have to get rid of anyone who blocks your path. I don't know what you and my sister have in mind for Earl Whitney but to make it work you're going to have to be ruthless with no second thoughts. Can you be that kind of man?'

This time Latchman's voice didn't waver. 'Yes.'

Bradford let go of the lapels. 'Good. Now get dressed. We have two people to kill.'

26

Leona began to relax somewhat. Samuel had become used to the movement and bumps of the wagon and had stopped crying. He was sleeping in the carrier on her back.

The young woman looked to the sky. A new red sun was keeping company with a partial circle of fading white. For Leona, there was something magical about having the sun and moon together. The whole world seemed to be a fairy tale.

She looked backward and the fairy tale atmosphere shattered. 'Del, I think we're bein' followed.'

Del turned his head back quickly. 'There is a cloud of dust coming toward us. Three riders, I'd say.'

'Maybe they're just on their way to Prentiss. Mr Riley said it was a busy town.'

Leona's voice sounded doubtful.

Del shared the doubt. 'We'll find out!' He shouted at the two horses and began to use the reins as whips. The wagon picked up speed. Ribbons of dust began to shoot from the wheels.

Fear gripped the young woman. 'Del, those riders. They've got their horses in a gallop. They're comin' after us!'

'We can't keep ahead of 'em.' Del again yelled at the horses, this time out of desperation. He knew the animals couldn't run much faster. Samuel was beginning to cry. The baby's screams added even more to Del's sense of urgency.

'I got an idea,' he yelled at Leona. 'Hold on, we're making a turn.'

Del yanked the reins and guided the horses on to a rocky path, only barely wide enough to contain the wagon. After less than a quarter mile, they were surrounded by land that was black with charcoal-colored trees standing barren. Their charred limbs looked like demonic tentacles and for a moment, Leona reckoned that this must be what hell looked like.

'There was a fire here 'bout six weeks ago,' Del shouted. 'But it didn't jump the stream up ahead.'

Burgess stopped the wagon, set the brake, and jumped off. He helped Leona down, and then grabbed the rifle Horace had given him along with the box of ammo, which he put in the pocket of his jacket.

'Come on.' He grabbed Leona's hand. They headed to a row of boulders that ran along the wide stream and crouched behind the largest one.

Burgess stood up briefly and listened for anything he could hear over Samuel's crying and the bray of the stream behind him. 'Don't hear nothing. They're still a few minutes away. I got time.'

'Time for what?'

Del picked up the Henry. 'Those few scrawny trees out there ain't gonna provide no cover. I've got plenty of ammo. I'll run 'em off or kill 'em if I gotta.'

Burgess put the rifle down and began to yank the string off the box of ammo. Leona watched him while whispering comforting words to Samuel. She reached her hand back and caressed the baby's head.

A loud curse sounded over Samuel's crying.

'What's wrong, Del?'

'There ain't no ammo in this box, just stones!' Burgess flung the box on to the ground.

Leona looked at the small pebbles scattered all about. 'How could Mr Riley make a mistake like that?'

'It weren't no mistake! He fooled us on purpose, acted like he was our friend.'

'But why?'

'Don't know, but I know this: you gotta git outta here!'

'I can't!'

'You can! The stream is shallow. It won't even reach your knees at the deepest part. Cross over and head north. You'll come to a path pretty soon. Follow it. It'll take you to the Baxter place. Stay there. I'll come for you.'

'I'm not leaving you, Del!'

'You gotta, Leona. We both gotta think 'bout Samuel.'

Leona pressed her lips together and began to cry. Del put a hand on both of her shoulders. 'None of that, now. Come on. We both gotta be brave. Git moving.'

The couple quickly embraced, then Del watched as Leona walked down a slight incline and entered the stream. She began to cross at a steady gait. Samuel was no longer crying.

Del closed his eyes and quickly prayed for deliverance from his enemies. He remembered hearing a preacher say that while the world was a big place, God heard every prayer that was spoken. He hoped the preacher got it right.

The approaching sound of hoof beats caused him to look back toward the stream. He silently rebuked himself. He must not do that again, it would give away Leona's location.

A plan quickly formed in the young man's mind. Not much of a plan, but then he didn't have much time.

Three riders were coming toward

him, stirring up a black cloud of ashes. Del stood up and frantically looked sideways. He gestured downward with one hand. Hopefully, his enemies would think Leona was crouched down behind the boulder.

He stepped out from the boulders and stood holding the rifle across his chest. Del noted that the morning sky still held enough darkness to be of some small help in shielding Leona.

The three horsemen all made coarse remarks as they dismounted. Del felt another surge of encouragement. Off their steeds, the three men would have less view of the stream.

Del pointed the Henry at his three adversaries. 'Stop right there!'

Horace Riley laughed as he took a step forward. 'Whatcha ya gonna do, boy? Shoot us with one of those little tiny stones I put in that ammo box?'

'You're a lying snake, Horace Riley.'

The intensity of Del's voice unsettled the blacksmith. Because of his enormous size, few men had ever challenged him. He now felt shaken by the young man, who glared accusingly at him.

But he couldn't allow his uncertainty to show. Bradford Maltin was his only hope of holding on to his business, his life. He had to get the man what he wanted.

Riley gave a forced laugh before speaking. 'I'm jus' a lot smarter than ya are, boy. I gave ya that Henry, 'cause I knew ya'd stop to shoot it out when ya saw us following ya. I read ya like a book.'

Del's laugh wasn't forced. 'You ain't never read a book in your life, Riley.'

Horace could hear his two companions guffawing behind him. He wanted to say something back but couldn't think of a thing. The blacksmith stood flustered and confused.

Del took advantage of that confusion. 'You didn't keep much of an eye on me, Riley, or you would know I took along my own box of ammo. This gun is loaded for bear. Mr Maltin, Mr Latchman, we ain't never been introduced but I recognize you gents. I suggest you both ride off. You're keepin' bad company.'

Bradford Maltin smiled as he stepped in front of Horace. 'Guess you're right about the bad company, young man. Let's deal. Tell Leona to come out with — '

'I see her!' Latchman yelled. 'She's on the other side of the stream!'

Bradford glanced in the direction Latchman was pointing. He began to run toward the stream. Del tripped the businessman, who dropped to his knees but quickly propelled himself up.

The monstrous apparition that was Horace Riley suddenly stood between Del and Bradford. The blacksmith's eyes were fermenting with hatred. 'Think you're smarter than me, boy?' Riley grabbed the rifle from Del's hands and tossed it away. 'That head of yours needs some straightening!'

Del ducked under Riley's swing and danced backwards. His opponent was stronger but slower. Del made a quick move to the blacksmith's side and delivered a hard rabbit punch under the big man's left eye.

Riley was an experienced fighter and knew he was up against an amateur. He staggered backwards as if his brain was twirling. Del moved in to deliver a fast series of knock-out punches.

The young man's vision blurred as a hard force slammed against his head. The earth seemed to wobble and suddenly Del's neck was caught in a powerful vice created by Riley's arm.

The young man struggled to breathe. He was stooped over, his head in a hammerlock, his neck pressed against Riley's side.

'I don't think ya'll be reading many more books yourself, boy.' Riley rammed Del's face with his left fist.

Del's vision blurred and dizziness filled his head. Through the buzz in his ears he could hear John Latchman shouting, 'That's enough. Stop, man! You'll kill him!'

'What's gotten into you, Latchman?' Riley's question was quickly answered by the sound of hoof beats. The sheriff and Rance Dehner pulled up and dismounted, guns drawn.

Riley let his prisoner loose and glanced about hurriedly for his horse. The two lawmen stood between him and his steed; there was no chance of making a run for it.

'Thank God you men are here!' Latchman proclaimed. 'I've been trying to stop this brute from beating this poor kid to death!'

'You lying snake!' Riley shouted at the lawyer, forgetting that Del Burgess had hurled the same accusation at him only moments before.

Latchman looked at the two lawmen. His dignified demeanor was shattered and his panic evident. 'Mr Maltin asked me to accompany him on what could become a complicated legal matter. I don't know why he brought along this blacksmith, I certainly did not — '

Amos Santell cut in on the lawyer's fast barrage of words. 'Make your fancy explanations later, Counselor. Right now, I want ya and the blacksmith, as ya call him, to put up your hands.'

Both men complied. Dehner approached Del Burgess who was staggering about. 'Are you OK, Del?'

'Never mind, me!' Del rasped. 'Leona, she's on other side of the stream . . . heading north. Maltin is after her . . . '

Dehner holstered his Colt, hurriedly jumped on to one of the boulders and used it to take a longer leap toward the stream. He ran down the short incline and paused only briefly to note the mess of footprints left in the mud beside the water a few minutes before.

The detective began to run across the stream, silently cursing his own foolishness. A series of sinister schemes had surrounded him since his arrival in Hardin; schemes which led to murder. He had been unable to stop them because of his own myopic vision.

Another collage of muddy footprints greeted him at the other side of the water. Dehner began to plow through thick foliage as he followed traces of mud inland. The woods became less thick the further he got from the stream. He arrived at a path the dust of which had been recently disturbed.

He began to run down the path but slowed as he heard a woman's screams. The screams were accompanied by a man's yells and a baby's cries. The detective stopped and then bolted into a grove of trees beside the path. Leona had apparently detoured into the grove in an attempt to hide from her pursuer — an attempt that had not worked.

Dehner advanced quietly but quickly around the trees. Small varmints scampered out of his way, as the human voices became closer.

'Don't fight me, Leona! I'm taking Samuel. He's mine!'

'You're not touching him!'

Bradford Maltin and Leona were in a small clearing. The businessman's back was to Dehner. The young woman raised her voice. 'You'll have to kill me, Bradford Maltin! I'll never give up my baby! You'll have to kill me!'

Leona's screams had the desired

effect. Bradford's attention was focused completely on the young woman and the baby strapped to her back. He didn't hear Dehner's footsteps and looked shocked when the detective spun him around and hit him with a sweeping uppercut.

Bradford hit the ground but didn't stay there. He buoyed to his feet and advanced toward Dehner cautiously. He seemed to be assessing his opponent, his eyes boiling with intelligence and cunning.

As the two men circled each other, it occurred to Dehner that the surrounding trees allowed them about the space of a boxing ring. 'You came to Hardin to get Curt Tatum didn't you, Rance?'

'That's right.' The circling continued.

'Tatum's dead. So, why not leave? I'd be happy to buy your ticket. I'll even include some extra funds. A lot more *dinero* than that agency you work for will ever pay you for a job.'

'Thanks, but no thanks, I plan — '

Bradford charged without warning.

The two men stood close, exchanging vicious blows. A madness seeped from Bradford's eyes as his fists pounded at Dehner's ribs and face. The detective replied in kind. Bradford's punches began to lose their force and then he again hit the ground. He maintained consciousness but Bradford Maltin was defeated and he knew it.

'You deliver a mean punch, Dehner.' He sat up, placing his head in his hands.

A new sense of respect connected the two men, but Dehner remained wary. He had spotted the shoulder holster under his opponent's coat. 'You're a good fighter, Maltin. I thought my surprise punch would finish you. I was wrong, but then I've been wrong about a lot of things in this case.'

A baby's cries could be heard from behind the trees. Leona stepped out into the clearing. Apparently, she had been watching the fight and now felt free to join Dehner. But the woman didn't speak to the detective. She unstrapped Samuel from her back and began to cradle the baby in her arms.

Bradford stared at the infant with longing and resignation. He looked disoriented as if waking from a dream and unsure of what constituted reality. He glanced back at Dehner and looked surprised to see him.

The businessman gave a mirthless laugh. 'Tell me, Dehner, what did you mean when you said you were wrong about a lot of things in this case?'

He remained sitting on the ground. Dehner continued to watch him carefully.

'I should have solved this case a few days after arriving in town.' The detective's voice revealed an anger with himself.

'Whaddya mean?' Leona asked as she rocked Samuel in her arms. The baby was no longer crying.

'There was so much money involved,' Dehner replied. 'Curt Tatum, Ash Carrick. Those gunslicks charge high. And I'd bet the Slocum brothers didn't come cheap. Rose Whitney was very open about the fact that her older brother was rich and, of course, the Whitneys are far from poor. I should have suspected Rose and Bradford immediately, just as a matter of routine.'

'So, why didn't you?' Bradford asked.

'There was nothing to gain by killing Leona,' Dehner answered. 'That is, nothing to gain monetarily. But, for once, you weren't thinking about money, were you, Bradford?'

Maltin's face began to soften. He seemed relieved to have found someone who understood his motives. 'Go ahead, Dehner, you're doing OK so far.'

'I listened in on your conversation with John Latchman earlier this evening. You want immortality, Bradford. You've built an empire and now you want to raise a grandson, someone with your blood in his veins who will make sure that your name lives forever.'

'I had someone like that, a son.' Bradford's voice choked, then he continued. 'Brad was my first born. I raised him to be a man; took him hunting, taught him how to shoot, swim . . . saw to it that he had boxing lessons. He was a terrific boy . . . then . . .'

'Will told me 'bout his older brother, Mr Maltin. How he died savin' him from drownin'. You can be very proud of Brad, Mr Maltin.'

'I am!' Bradford Maltin lifted his voice; a fierce energy seemed to quickly surge through him and then vanish, leaving him limp.

The businessman slowly rose to his feet. 'These woods are beautiful.'

A heightened tension shot through Rance Dehner. 'Maltin, I want you to put your hands up and leave them there while I take your gun.'

'Brad loved the outdoors,' Bradford continued as if his captor hadn't spoken. 'He died outdoors in a lake where we had gone swimming together, fished together.'

'I said put your hands up, Maltin.'

'Sorry, Dehner, I'm going for my gun. You're going to have to kill me.'

'Bradford, no — '

'I'm going to die in the outdoors, just like my son. I'm not going to hang, become a spectacle, like a freak in some cheap circus.'

'I'm telling you for the last time, Bradford, put your hands up.'

'And I'm telling you for the last time, Dehner, I'm going for my gun. If you don't kill me, I'll kill you, then I'll kill the girl and take Samuel. It's your choice.'

He reached for his gun. Dehner drew his Colt and sent a bullet into Bradford Maltin's chest.

The businessman collapsed to the ground for the last time as Leona gave a loud scream. Birds flew away noisily as if distancing themselves from the repulsive creatures below. Dehner walked over to the corpse, and mechanically picked up Maltin's wrist feeling for a pulse that wasn't there.

Leona sobbed as she rocked a frightened baby in her arms.

27

Samuel was once again riding on Leona's back as the young woman and Dehner neared the end of the path and approached a tangle of trees and foliage that led to water. They both stopped as the sound of a gunshot roared over the gurgling of the nearby stream.

'Amos is having trouble with his prisoners,' Dehner snapped.

Leona's voice was close to a cry. 'Del, I hope Del hasn't been hurt.'

Dehner immediately took on a more calm demeanor. 'Del is OK. There is nothing to worry about. Amos Santell is the only person there holding a gun. If he shot someone it was Riley or Latchman. Both of them deserve it.'

Leona seemed to calm down a bit. Dehner hoped his words were true. He had not told the girl about Del taking a beating from Horace Riley and this was not the time to do so.

The detective took Leona's hand and they made it cautiously through the thickets, taking care that Samuel didn't get scratched. Dehner entered the stream first. A little less than halfway across he drew his Colt. He could see some movement from the people on shore but couldn't make out what was happening.

As they left the water, Leona began to run toward the men on shore, anxious to see if Del was OK. Dehner didn't even try to hold her back. He contented himself to run in front of her, gun drawn.

The detective holstered his gun as they got closer to the men. Sheriff Santell was crouched over Horace Riley, putting a bandanna on his shoulder. Del stood beside the lawman, holding a gun on Riley.

Del looked anxious as he spotted the detective running toward him, then happiness and relief flared in his face as he saw Leona. He handed the gun to

Dehner and embraced the young woman. Both he and Leona tried not to cry. They had little success in that endeavor but the sobs soon became laughter. The couple began to assure each other that they were all right.

'We're together now, Leona,' Del said. 'We ain't never gonna part again until the good Lord calls one of us home.'

Dehner smiled at those words. He believed what Del Burgess said and for the first time since this case began, the detective felt content.

Amos Santell glared at the temporary bandage he had put on his prisoner. 'That should keep you 'til we get back to town and the sawbones.' The lawman arose from his crouch. 'No more tomfoolery. One bandanna is enough to waste on the likes of you.'

Dehner handed the sheriff his gun. 'What happened? Where's John Latchman?'

Amos smirked, primarily to himself. 'While you were gone, Del collapsed.'

The sheriff pointed his gun accusingly at Horace Riley. 'This galoot had hit the boy pretty hard. John Latchman walked over and started to help the kid up by one arm but Del was havin' trouble stayin' on his feet. I walked over and grabbed the other arm. 'Fore you know it, Latchman has pushed me to the ground and put a boot to my ribs, then Riley is standin' over me, gettin' ready for an attack. I didn't take no chances with that monster. I put a bullet in Horace's shoulder.'

'Latchman got away?'

Amos sighed and smiled in a sheepish manner. 'Yeah. Rode off. Don't know where he went to.'

Dehner did know. 'Can you handle things here OK?'

'Sure.' Santell looked down at his prisoner. 'Havin' a bullet in his shoulder has given Horace a more gentle temperament.'

Dehner ran for his horse. He knew where Latchman was headed. He didn't feel content anymore.

John Latchman rode on to the Whitney ranch and into a swarm of activity. Breakfast was over. Men were starting the day's work. None of the ranch-hands paid any attention to him. If they had, they would have noticed that his hands were trembling and his face was pale with desperation.

As he dismounted, the lawyer looked with anger and hatred toward a group of cowboys who, it appeared, were riding off to do repairs on a fence. Only yesterday Latchman had felt vastly superior to such common folks. He stood above the masses who were destined to spend their lives getting their hands dirty from hard work. Now he realized the raw-boned cow hands starting their day of work could be part of a posse that would be coming after him.

Latchman tethered his horse at a rail in front of the house. Well, let them come. They'd never get him. John Latchman was superior to them all. He would find another town somewhere far away and become a king as he would have in Hardin if only a stupid sheriff and some out of town detective hadn't gotten lucky.

He pulled a Winchester from the boot of his saddle. The lawyer had already killed one man for Rose Whitney and now he would kill another. Latchman couldn't go on without Rose and believed she loved and needed him.

A man carrying a rifle at a large ranch was hardly an unusual sight. The few cowboys who glanced at John Latchman stepping on to the porch of the ranch house thought nothing of it.

Latchman pounded on the front door. Earl Whitney opened it with a look of curiosity laced with anger. 'Good morning, Mr Latchman. What brings you here?'

'I have to see Rose.'

'And just why do you have to see my wife?'

'I said I have to see Rose!' Latchman pushed Earl back and stepped inside

271

closing the door.

But shoving Earl Whitney had been harder and more dangerous than he anticipated. Whitney took a step toward the intruder. 'Just what do you think you're doing?'

Rose Whitney entered the living room. 'What's going on?'

Latchman pointed the Winchester directly at Earl. 'We have to run from this place, Rose. Everything has fallen apart. Your brother is probably heading for jail right now. It's only a matter of time before that detective pieces everything together. They'll be coming after us!'

Panic shot through Rose Whitney but she quickly tamped it down. She had to assume that Latchman was speaking the truth. Bradford's plans had, somehow, been exposed. Maybe her brother would hang. She wouldn't. Earl Whitney was her road out of this dilemma.

She gave her husband an astonished look and then spoke to the man who was pointing a rifle at him. 'I don't have the slightest idea what you're talking about.'

It was Latchman's turn to look astonished. 'I'm talking about the fact that I killed Ash Carrick for you, Rose. You needed him dead because he could expose you as the one who hired him to kill Leona.'

'You're insane!' Rose shouted at John Latchman, but the words were for her husband.

Earl Whitney took another step toward the lawyer. Latchman raised the Winchester in a threatening manner. 'We've got to run from here, Rose. Throw some things in a bag. I'll kill this old fool and then we'll run. We'll start fresh in a new town far away . . . '

The lawyer's voice took on a pleading quality as he turned to face Rose. Earl moved with panther speed, slamming a fist into Latchman's jaw. Latchman staggered backwards and in a panicked reflex fired the rifle.

A woman's brief scream was followed by the sound of Rose crumpling to the floor. Earl ran to his fallen wife and dropped to his knees beside her. He placed two fingers on her neck. 'You've killed her.' He rose to his feet. 'You've killed my wife.'

The two men faced each other, a look of stunned horror on both of their faces. John Latchman stepped hesitantly toward the body that lay on the floor. As he looked down on the corpse of the woman he had killed and killed for, his face twisted and he screamed at Earl Whitney, 'You murdered her! If you hadn't hit me, I never — '

Latchman levered the Winchester as the front door flew open and Rance Dehner yelled, 'Drop the rifle, right now!'

This time, the lawyer didn't turn his head. He knew his life was over and didn't care. But John Latchman had one more deed to perform. He gave Earl Whitney a glare of raw hatred. 'You're travelling to hell with me!'

Dehner's bullet cut into Latchman's head as he began to exert pressure on the trigger of the Winchester. The lawyer's body heaved sideways and dropped to the ground as the rifle fired into the grand piano that filled much of the room. Wild screeches accompanied the gunfire like the bellows of a mythical dragon.

And then there was silence. Dehner walked cautiously toward the body of John Latchman and crouched over it to ensure that the man was dead. Latchman would be journeying to hell by himself, the detective thought, but he said nothing. He arose and faced Earl Whitney, who seemed to be in a private hell of his own.

The rancher stood staring out the front window at a group of men running toward the house. He turned to the detective. 'What that madman just said about Rose hiring men to kill, it was . . . insanity.'

'Yes,' Dehner replied.

Hard fists assaulted the front door. 'Mr Whitney! Mr Whitney! Everythin' OK in there?'

'Could you handle all of this?' Earl spoke in a trembling whisper. 'I need to be alone for a while.'

'Yes, of course, is there anyone I can get for you, someone who — '

'No, there's no one.' Earl Whitney walked off by himself.

28

Rance Dehner left Hardin, Texas the next day. While he joked a bit with Amos Santell and Max Chumley before leaving, the trip back to Dallas was filled with hard, unpleasant notions.

He kept trying to tell himself that he had accomplished his aims. Curt Tatum was gone and, more important, Leona and her son were safe.

But so many people had been killed during his stay in Hardin. Yes, most of them were people who needed killing. The world would not mourn the loss of Ash Carrick, John Latchman, or the Slocum brothers.

In all likelihood, Reverend Jeremy Lanning had been a good man. But Dehner knew he had become involved with the case far too late to have saved the pastor.

On the second night of his journey,

Dehner sat by the camp-fire, staring at an angry dark sky. Bradford Maltin had been a special case, he mused to himself. The detective felt he had not really killed the businessman but rather helped him to commit suicide. Maltin wanted to die because he could not have the one thing that was still important to him: an heir. He wanted someone who could carry on his work and carry on his name. And, he couldn't face becoming a 'spectacle' at a hanging.

A light raindrop fell into Dehner's coffee cup. The detective sipped from the cup and thought about Rose Whitney. Perhaps her death was merciful. Rose was an accomplice in the killing of Ash Carrick and, Dehner suspected, Reverend Lanning. If her case had gone to court, it probably would have been established that she was assisting her brother in trying to kill Leona Carson. Rose Whitney could have become a historical figure: one of the few women in the West to die by a rope.

Now, there would be no trial. All of

the culprits were dead except Horace Riley, a small fish who knew nothing about the bigger picture. Earl Whitney wouldn't have to listen to any accusations against his wife. He could keep his illusions.

How much did Earl Whitney really believe those noble thoughts about his wife? The detective didn't know but figured Mr Whitney held tight to his illusions because to do otherwise would lead to unbearable pain.

'We do what we have to in order to survive,' Dehner said out loud.

The rain began to fall harder.

* * *

Two years later, Dehner received a letter from Will Maltin, which was addressed in care of the Lowrie Detective Agency.

Dear Mr Dehner
During our brief meeting two years ago, I came to appreciate that you are a man of great competence and discretion. You are a gentleman. Therefore,

I am confident I can entrust you with the following matter.

I am now employed by the company once owned by my father. I have risen to a prominent position with a commensurate salary and can now make amends for an earlier indiscretion.

I am aware that Del Burgess planned to marry Leona. They were going to leave Hardin and start a new life where they could raise Samuel free of wagging tongues.

Such a course of action is laudable and I wish to provide financial assistance. My plan is to send them three hundred dollars every year at Christmas. Of course, the gift will be anonymous.

Please be assured that I do not intend to cause any trouble for Mr and Mrs Burgess or to make any claims on Samuel. I am now courting a woman of appropriate station in life and realize the foolishness of my earlier dalliance. Nevertheless, I am a man of honor.

I wish to engage you to find out where Del and Leona Burgess are now living *and provide me with the address where I can send the money. Enclosed is a cheque. Please let me know if the sum is adequate.*

Thank you for the efforts of your good offices.

Dehner returned the cheque along with the address, which he already knew. He felt confident that Will was telling the truth. He wouldn't cause Del and Leona any problems.

The detective had recently passed through the town where the young couple now lived. Del was busy establishing his own blacksmith business; Leona was expecting their second child. That yearly Christmas gift would come in handy.

But Will's writing had left the detective uneasy. An aristocratic arrogance tinged the letter. It was the writing of a man who always expected to get his way.

A coldness seized the detective. Will Maltin was becoming like his father. Instead of going on a killing spree to gain control of Samuel, Bradford

Maltin needed only to have focused on his younger son to have the heir he so desperately wanted. All of that killing had been unnecessary.

The coldness remained with Dehner for the rest of the day and well into the night.

* * *

Three months later, Dehner scurried into his Dallas office early. He was leaving that morning for Arizona and a murder case that awaited him there. The letter that lay on his desk bore a woman's handwriting and an unfamiliar return address. He grabbed a letter opener and ripped the envelope with a quick, indifferent stroke. As he began to read, his indifference vanished.

Dear Mr Dehner
You remember me, if you remember me at all, as June Day. I was a saloon girl you encountered in Hardin, Texas over two years ago. I hope this

letter finds you well.

I wanted to write you earlier but did not know your address. I did know the address of Amos Santell and wrote dear Amos asking him for assistance. You will not be surprised to learn that Sheriff Santell was slow in responding but when he did write, his letter was long and informative.

The sheriff wrote that his deputy has become a 'love-sick fool' over the daughter of a preacher who arrived in Hardin about eighteen months ago. Max will be getting married soon. I was happy to hear that. Max is a wonderful young man who was very lonely. (Men tell things to saloon girls that they would tell to no one else.)

As for Amos, well, he and Earl Whitney have frequent checker games together. What's more, Mr Whitney is teaching the sheriff how to play chess. According to Amos, chess is a much more 'high hat' game than checkers.

Now to my purpose in writing.

Thank you, thank you, for encouraging me to return to my husband. I had not fully appreciated what a wonderful man I was married to. He welcomed me back eagerly and forgave my unfaithfulness.

I would never have even tried to return to Harold Preston if you had not challenged me to do so. I have chosen to express my deep appreciation in a unique way. Our son, now eight months of age, is named Harold Rance Preston.

It is my hope that someday you will meet Harold Rance Preston and his father. I have told my husband much about you and he has asked me to send you his gratitude for bringing me to my senses.

But, if we don't meet again in this life, please know that you have brought untold happiness to the Preston family. May God bless you.

The letter was signed June Preston. June Day was gone forever. Good.

Dehner carefully placed the letter in the top drawer of his desk. He had no idea if he would ever see June Preston again. But her letter would be a keepsake; a reminder of the impact one man can have on the lives of people he encounters for only a short time.

Rance Dehner felt good as he left for Arizona and another case.

We do hope that you have enjoyed reading this large print book.

Did you know that all of our titles are available for purchase?

We publish a wide range of high quality large print books including:
Romances, Mysteries, Classics
General Fiction
Non Fiction and Westerns

Special interest titles available in large print are:
The Little Oxford Dictionary
Music Book, Song Book
Hymn Book, Service Book

Also available from us courtesy of Oxford University Press:
Young Readers' Dictionary
(large print edition)
Young Readers' Thesaurus
(large print edition)

For further information or a free brochure, please contact us at:
Ulverscroft Large Print Books Ltd.,
The Green, Bradgate Road, Anstey,
Leicester, LE7 7FU, England.
Tel: (00 44) **0116 236 4325**
Fax: (00 44) **0116 234 0205**

DERBY JOHN'S ALIBI

Ethan Flagg

Derby John Daggert is out for revenge on his employer after a severe beating meted out for theft and adultery. Then a robbery goes badly wrong, two men are murdered, and the killer makes a wild ride from Querida to Denver. As prime suspect, Daggert is arrested, but his lawyer convinces the jury he was elsewhere when the crime was committed. It is left to Buckskin Joe Swann to hunt down the culprit — a task more difficult than he could have ever imagined . . .

HOOD

Jake Douglas

When he wakes wounded in the badlands, he doesn't even know his own name, where he is, or how he got there. He sure doesn't know who shot him and left him to die. But when the riders come to try and finish the job, they call him 'Hood' . . . Under the scorching sun, he does the only thing he can: straps on a six-gun, gets back in the saddle, and sets out to find out who's on his trail . . .